# I,
# Vampire

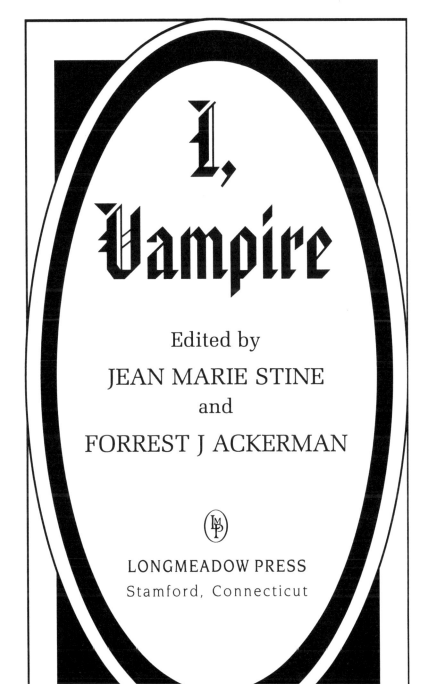

# I, Vampire

### Edited by

## JEAN MARIE STINE
### and
## FORREST J ACKERMAN

LONGMEADOW PRESS

Stamford, Connecticut

Published by Longmeadow Press, 201 High Ridge Road, Stamford, Connecticut 06904. All rights reserved. No part of this book may be reproduced or utilized in any form or by any means, electronic or mechanical, including photocopying, recording or by any information storage or retrieval system, without permission in writing from the Publisher. Longmeadow Press and the colophon are trademarks.

Cover and interior design by Pamela C. Pia.

Jacket illustration Copyright © 1994 by Alan Clark.

Library of Congress Cataloging-in-Publication Data
I, Vampire / edited by Jean Stine and Forrest J Ackerman.
— 1st Longmeadow Press ed.
    p.  cm.
  ISBN 0-681-00798-2
    1. Vampires—Fiction.   2. Short stories, American.   I. Stine, Jean
Marie.   II. Ackerman, Forrest J
PS648.V35I2   1995
813'.0108375—dc20                                        95-6075
                                                          CIP

Printed and bound in the United States of America.
First Longmeadow Press edition.
0 9 8 7 6 5 4 3 2 1

# Dedication

*To*
Bram Stoker
Bela Lugosi
Christopher Lee
*&*
All Those Other Wonderful People
Who Frightened Us To Death

# Contents

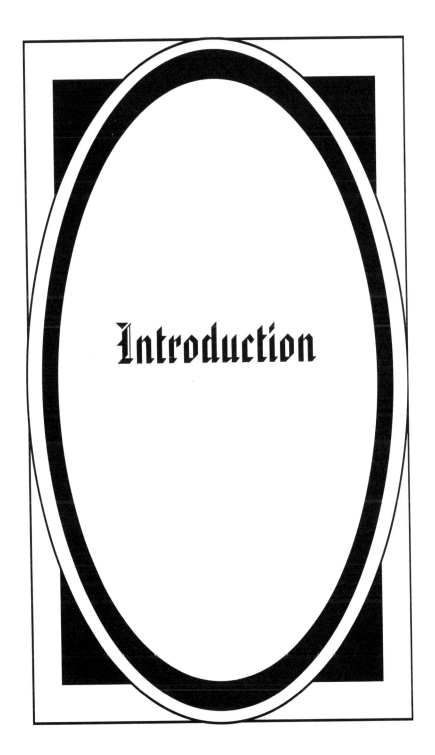

Introduction

# Introduction

MEET THE VAMPIRES!

For eons these denizens of the night have avoided human contact and shrouded themselves in secrecy.

Today they are coming out of the closet along with everyone else. The worst are seen as helpless victims of an obsessive-compulsive disorder, driven by an irresistible craving for blood. The best, as noble figures who fight against this terrible craving, constantly seeking ways to overcome it, while suffering guilt every time they are forced to give in.

Instead of wanting to terrify us, this new breed of vampires simply wants to tell us their stories. Instead of our blood, they want our understanding—even our forgiveness. Instead of taking our lives, they want to take our time.

And we let them.

Why?

Through out all recorded history, people have been fascinated by vampires. This fascination seems to be part and parcel of our fascination with death, dying and the mysterious unknown that lies beyond. Legends of undead creatures that return to life in the dark of night to feed on the living have been with us since the dawn of time.

Not only does every culture have its variant, but tales of vampires are found on continents so widely scattered the stories can have no single common origin. Undoubtedly graves disturbed by wild animals and the many wasting sicknesses of ancient times account for most of these stories. More human monsters, still very much among the living, who fed upon the blood of their fellow mortals for the simple power or cruelty of it, probably account for the rest.

Put this way, there seems to be nothing glamorous about vampires. And yet, the undead alone, of all the monsters that have haunted humankind, have exerted an enormous appeal over the popular imagination. The number of great novels about werewolves can be counted on one hand (without using all five fingers). The number of great vampire novels stretches from Varney to Dracula to Saint-Germain.

Perhaps more to the point, we are not merely fascinated by vampires—we envy them. How else can we explain the enduring popularity of the infamous Count and his ken. Undead, unbound by the constraints of social or physical laws, they are free to be everything we have been inculcated *not* to be: openly evil, openly sexual, openly powerful. Not to mention they possess some very nifty supernatural abilities: they can impose their will on others; enter any building by turning into mist; command the elements; mesmerize members of the gender they prefer most; transform themselves into bats, wolves and other creatures at a moment's notice; and best of all (when we were little kids), they sleep by day and party all night.

When the vampire got staked at the end of the story, we were always a little sad to see him (or her) go—for a little of us went with them. We may have wanted the hero and heroine to escape—but, secretly, we wished we were the vampire. We might have imagined we'd solve the blood problem by feasting on bovine hemoglobin, raiding blood banks or doing away with those the world could do without. But it was the vampire we were one with, the vampire we wanted to be, the vampire at the center of the story—not its boring, puny human protagonists.

Still, vampires were the bad guys, and we had to hide our fondness for (our desire to be) them. It was one of those shameful vices, like self-gratification, we felt we must conceal from the disapproving scrutiny of the world-at-large. To admit we identified with a blood-sucking demon who rose from her (or his) grave every night, would have marked us indelibly as "seriously weird" in the eyes of others.

Yet women swooned when Bela Lugosi's eyes glowed hypnotic from the screen; and did so again, when Christopher Lee's optics performed similar perambulations. While men tingled to be fanged by any number of celluloid vampiresses, from Gloria Holden to Barbara Shelly.

Then in a moment of desperation, Dan Curtis and Art Wallace, their boringly traditional gothic soap opera stalled in the afternoon ratings basement, introduced a vampire meant to be menacing. But when the actor's haunted delivery came across with more torment than menace, millions of fan letters began to pour in. The producers quickly shifted story-line, suddenly their vampire was no longer the shallow blood-sucker he'd started as in the early episodes. Now, he was a sensitive, Byronic hero, brooding eternally over the lives he was forced to take and the woman he had loved and lost centuries before.

The vampire as protagonist (and often as hero or heroine) was born. Previous vampires like Dracula had gloried in blood-lust and slaughter, relishing the moment when they drew thirst-quenching life from their victim's throats. The new breed of vampire carried the angst of the modern world on their shoulders. Here, was clearly a vampire for contemporary times— one whose basic problem, an irresistible compulsion to a self-destructive act, was shared in some form by everyone.

Given "good guy" (and gal) vampires, vampire lovers everywhere came out of the closet. The soap, *Dark Shadows*, became a world-celebrated success, and soon authors like Anne Rice, inspired by its example, began creating sympathetic vampires of their own. The world was hit by a flood of novels, stories, collections, movies and television programs about vampiric protagonists who are just like "thee and me" (though a bit nobler) in every way but one. And for the most part they are just as disturbed by that difference as we would be, and struggle just as hard to overcome it as we would.

Plus these modern vampires possess all those wonderful powers we always envied—without having to be evil, exactly. No wonder we have fallen for these likable undead by the dozens. They enable us to enjoy our vampiric fantasies— guilt-free.

We have invited them into our homes, asked them to sit by the hearth, pressed them to tell us their stories. And Lestat and his legions have responded. Of course, not all of the undead have proved exemplary characters—and not all of our interviews with them have proved so pleasant.

Yet each encounter teaches us something about what it means to be dead and something about what it means to be alive. For vampires, the best and the worst, are only our human characteristics exaggerated: the way we feed on other forms of life, the way we drain energy from those around us, our greed, our violence, the way we selfishly put our own survival above all else. Their stories are only our stories writ large, seen "in a glass darkly"—but the reflection they hold up is true.

No wonder the undead fascinate us so much. To paraphrase one of our greatest philosophers: We have met vampires, and they are us!

So here are twelve never before heard interviews with today's undead, each conducted by one of our leading contemporary reporters on the bizarre, the fantastic and the strange and each written especially for this book. In each, the undead are allowed to tell their own stories uncensored and in their own words. Some of their tales are touching, some comic, some chilling, some deeply disturbing. But all offer us vital insights into the darker aspects of our times and our selves.

Fangs for the memories!

Forrest J Ackerman
Jean Marie Stine
Hollywood, California
1995

# I,
# Vampire

# By Moonlight

## JOHN GREGORY BETANCOURT

*"Know thy self"*
*may not*
*always be*
*the best*
*advice.*

VEN BY MOONLIGHT, the farm looked like a disaster area.

The barn had started to lean, so much paint had peeled off the main building that its walls looked like sun-bleached driftwood, and at least half of the outbuildings had collapsed. I drove forward slowly, my rental car nosing among the scattered clumps of rusted-out machinery like a reluctant explorer, until I reached the house's front step

They say you always come full circle, but it was hard to believe I'd spent the first eighteen years of my life here. How long ago had it been now? I thought hard and couldn't remember today's date, not the year anyway. Nineteen ninety something. August 14, I thought. Time didn't mean much anymore.

It had been at least fifty years since I'd seen this place.

Returning for my father's funeral had been hard enough; I'd hoped driving out to the farm one last time would be easier. *I could have prevented it. I could have made him one like me. He didn't need to die.*

But he would have wanted it this way, him with his

unsmiling Christian ways.

I had an uneasy feeling, like I'd returned to the scene of some crime I'd committed, but of course that couldn't be true. I'd always been careful to cover my tracks; nobody could ever follow me here. Was it guilt? I could have laughed. My kind didn't feel guilt. Nevertheless I had the vague feeling I'd betrayed someone, left some promise unfulfilled.

Shutting off the car's engine, I climbed out and paused, turning slowly, listening to the wind in the fields and the hum of insects. My darker senses took in the whole of the land around me, cataloging the living and the dead. *A few gophers, a stray dog prowling the gully behind the house, birds drowsing safely in their nests, a snake languorously swallowing a mouse* . . . And, farther away at the next, farm over—old Man Jessup's place, but he'd be long gone by now—young lovers sat on the front porch, holding hands, kissing. I could feel the rising intensity of their passion.

Abruptly I called in my vision. Business first, I thought. I walked up the creaking old steps to the front door and pulled out the key. The lock clicked, the door opened easily, and a musty, stale smell hit me in the face. I wrinkled my nose and stepped in.

The carpets were dirty and worn through in places, the wallpaper was peeling, and the furniture looked broken and tattered. Even so, a lump rose in my throat. Less than I'd thought had changed in the years since I'd left,

"Home," I whispered.

I'd been born in this house, lived my first eighteen years here, and only escaped when I'd been drafted into the war . . .

THE NIGHT IN 1944 when the German artillery shot my bomber down, we'd already dumped our cargo over Dresden.

JOHN GREGORY BETANCOURT

I had watched the city burning below and felt a vindictive sort of pride: *take that, you bastards,* I thought. *For all the suffering, for all the innocents you've killed or enslaved, for all the terror and fear and death you caused, take that!*

Suddenly the plane lurched, but it wasn't like hitting an air pocket. We fell to the side—my buddy Lou on top of me, both of us all knees and elbows as we tried to right ourselves—and when we couldn't, I realized it was because the plane had tilted. We lurched again, and suddenly wind screamed in, along with an oily black smoke that made me gasp for breath.

"Come on!" Lou shouted in my ear, and somehow we made it to the hatch. He blew it open and pushed me out.

I don't remember much after that. I think I must've hit my head. Somehow, though, my parachute opened and I made it to the ground safely, instinctively tucking and rolling like I'd drilled to do so many times.

When I came up to my feet, several bright lights suddenly shone in my eyes. I raised a hand to shield my face, blind, afraid. Squinting, I made out half a dozen men in German uniforms with rifles leveled at my chest. I raised my hands. Their captain drew a large knife and stepped forward. I tensed, but he only cut the parachute away. Then he searched me and confiscated my pistol, knife, and survival kit. He tucked my cigarettes into his pocket and handed my wallet back after flipping through it once. I don't think the pictures of my mother and father interested him.

"*Namen?*" he asked, pulling out a little black book.

"Private Anderson, Tucker," I said, and recited my serial number. He jotted it down, then put his book away.

"You are prisoner," he said in heavily accented English. "Come now."

Turning, he led the way to a dirt road, where a dusty old truck waited. At his gesture, two of his men lowered the clapboard. I climbed in past two alert looking guards.

"No talk," said the captain who'd found me. Then his boots crunched on the ground and he was gone.

I leaned forward, straining to see my fellow prisoners. Had the Germans caught Lou? As best I could tell in the darkness, about half a dozen sullen men sat there with me. One of then moaned a little. I could smell blood and urine.

"Hello?" I whispered. "Lou?"

"Shh," the man next to me said softly in my ear. "The guards will give you a thrashing if they hear." He had a British accent. "We're all RAF," he added. "No other yanks in here, old boy."

"Thanks," I whispered.

"Smithers," he said softly, and we shook hands.

"Tuck," I told him.

He nodded and that was the end of it. I sank back a little. Lou wasn't here. He might have gotten away.

It was a small comfort.

IT WAS DAWN when the truck started. By the thin gray morning light, I could see my five fellow prisoners clearly for the first time. They looked as bleary-eyed and miserable as I felt. Smithers was a corporal, I saw. Nobody said anything; we just rode in a sullen, helpless silence under the watchful eyes of our two guards.

After an hour or so, we came to a stop. Through the back of the truck I could see what looked like a small rail yard. Dense forest came down near the trucks about a hundred yards away. The guards lowered the clapboard and motioned us out. Stretching stiff muscles, we complied.

Several boxcars were parked on the tracks waiting for an

engine, I saw. The guards lined us up while they opened one, then loaded us into it like cattle. Dirty straw lined the floor, I saw when I stepped in. It smelled faintly of mold.

"What about a doctor?" Smithers called to the captain outside. "Can you get us a doctor? One of our chaps has a broken arm! You there—"

The guards rolled the boxcar's door shut with a firm thump and I heard a bar being lowered into place. Luckily it wasn't dark inside. Blades of light slanted between the thick wooden slats of the walls.

"Hey!" Smithers yelled.

I heard boots walking away. We were alone.

"Bastards," Smithers swore. He kicked the door for a little while, but it did no good.

Everyone else was settling down on the straw. I hadn't realized how drained I was; when I lay down, I fell asleep almost at once, but not easily and not deeply.

TWICE THAT DAY the guards opened the door, once to serve a kind of lunch—a thin greasy stew and stale bread—and once to replace the latrine bucket in the corner. Each time Smithers tried to talk to the Germans about Carter, the man with the broken arm, but they either didn't understand or weren't interested in anything but their immediate task.

There didn't seem to be much else we could do but make the poor devil comfortable. Carter seemed in a kind of fever dream, talking or moaning every now and again, sometimes thrashing about, and I thought that sleep was probably the best thing for him. He wouldn't be aware of his pain. We took turns sitting beside him, talking soothingly if he moaned, trying to make him as comfortable as we could. He seemed to be growing steadily worse despite everything we did.

"He'll be dead by morning," I heard one of the men mutter.

Smithers shot him an angry look. "None of that," he said. "He's a strong lad, our Carter. He'll pull through."

That evening the Germans served the same sort of greasy stew again, and after we finished, they brought in another three British prisoners. I wondered if that was a good or a bad sign for my friend Lou.

Darkness fell, and I began to feel sleepy even though I'd spent most of the day half drowsing out on the straw. I stretched out and began to drift off.

Suddenly Carter thrashed like a crazed mule. His boot struck me in the arm, and cursing, I sat up and pinned his legs to protect myself.

"Easy there," I murmured. "Easy." At last he lay still, panting. I arranged the straw under his head, then looked at the others.

None of them had moved a muscle to help. I shook my head. Carter was one of theirs. They should be the ones looking after him, I thought, not me. A few seconds later Carter lay quietly again. Everyone else was snoring softly. Rising, I moved to the other end of the boxcar. He wouldn't wake me up again tonight, I thought. If he cried out, one of his mates could see to him.

Then I heard the bar on the door lift, and rollers squealed as the door moved aside. A dark shape stood silhouetted in the opening. It moved forward, snuffling the air like a pig. At once it drifted to the injured man, hunched over him, and a soft lapping sound began.

I had to be dreaming, I thought. I rubbed my eyes, but the door still gaped and the creature still crouched over Carter. Everyone else still seemed to be asleep. I touched my sore arm. I would have been asleep, too, I thought, if Carter hadn't

JOHN GREGORY BETANCOURT

kicked me.

Moving as softly as I could, taking great care not to rustle the straw, I crept up on the stranger. At the time I thought he must have heard me, but now I know he sensed my aliveness behind him. As I was about to jump forward, he suddenly rose and whirled, and I gazed into a face from a madman's nightmare.

He had eyes that glowed like a cat's, only red, and fangs like a snake's. Blood covered his face and hands. As I watched, a long thin white tongue licked it from his lips and chin.

Slowly he smiled. It was the most terrifying expression I had ever seen, and it sent a cold jolt through me, worse than anything I could ever have imagined. I felt my bladder let go. An icy sweat began to pour from my skin. I trembled. I shook all over. No matter how I tried, I could not look away from those horrible red eyes.

"Zo," it whispered, for I realized that it was not a man. "Was makst du hier, Mann?" It drifted forward like a cloud of smoke, enveloping me, and I blinked and found myself on my back. A numbness came over me. I heard the lapping sound again, but closer, at my throat. My mind drifted like a leaf in a stream.

AIR RAID SIRENS suddenly blew outside. I blinked and sat up, suddenly alone. My neck ached. My hands felt icy. My legs shook like gelatin.

With effort, I turned to look for the creature, but it seemed to have vanished. The boxcar's door still stood open. I crawled to it, then half fell out onto the train tracks. I huddled there for a moment, afraid I'd been seen or heard. Across from the boxcar I saw running men, and one by one windows in the station went dark. The air raid siren blared. Far overhead, I heard the throaty rumble of bombers.

Somehow, I climbed to my feet and stumbled off toward the forest. My only thought was of escape from the creature. If a German guard had found me, I think I would have embraced him with joy.

I must have been dazed by the attack, driven half crazy from fear and pain and bloodloss. As I think back over the months that followed, only fractured images come to mind: stalking small animals in the dark, ripping open their throats, drinking their blood to warm my cold insides. Hiding in a fox burrow against the painful brightness of day. Sobbing uncontrollably at the sight of towns, of distant men and women, of the kind of warm happy life I felt I had lost forever.

Whatever that creature was, whatever it had done to me, I realized that I, too, was no longer a man. I hunted and lived as an animal. And, like an animal, I began to rely on my senses—senses which now seemed inexplicably altered. As I moved silently through the forest, I could somehow feel every warm living body around me . . . could paralyze small animals with the force of my gaze . . . could hunt as the fiercest predators must have done in the dawn of history.

The first true memory I have is of taking a human life: a boy who wandered too far into the woods one night fell prey to my fangs. After I drank his life away, I recoiled in horror at what I had done, and it was as though I awakened for the first time since the Germans had captured me. *I had murdered a boy.* It was truly the worst moment of my life.

I buried him deep in my fox burrow and fled deep into the woods. That afternoon I sensed hundreds of men searching for the boy, felt their pain of loss, their hurt and despair. I longed to go to them, to tell them what I had done, to take my punishment like a man, but I could not summon the strength. They never found either of us.

After that I vowed not to give in to my base instincts. I would not be a wild creature unfit for human company. And so, very slowly, very painfully, with the death of that boy, I did gain a measure of control over myself.

It was as though I had emerged from a dream, or perhaps from an infancy of sorts. I came aware of myself and saw what I had become: a dirty, naked, monstrous beast sucking the life from the living. I could not continue this way.

Over the next few months I took greater care. After satisfying my hungers with the blood of beasts, I crept out of the forest and moved among the dwellings of men. Now that I tried, I discovered I could render whole households unconscious with the sheer force of my will. As they slept, I crept among them and took whatever I needed: soap, a razor, clean clothes, and their brightly colored paper money. The war must be over, I realized as I studied them in their beds. They had the soft, well-fed look of peace all about them.

When I caught sight of my reflection in a mirror, I knew the truth. I had not wanted to admit it, but inside I had already guessed what I had become: a vampire. Not one like Bela Lugosi's Dracula in the movies, cringing at crosses and holy water, but a man transformed into a blood-driven animal, with all of a man's weaknesses and an animal's strengths. I could not turn myself into an animal; I *was* an animal—a nocturnal, blood-drinking animal with powers over the minds and bodies of others—so much for legends, I thought. Crosses, garlic, and running water wouldn't stop me. I suspected bullets might.

Of course there were moments of self-pity, times when I wondered why I had been spared death to continue this monstrous half life. Why me? I silently cried. Why couldn't I have died in that boxcar so long ago? I had no answer.

I had avoided the sun, but the next day I went out in it. As

I suspected, I found it uncomfortable and far too bright, but my flesh did not burn. With dark glasses and a hat, I could move in the daytime if I chose.

I stole glasses and a hat that evening.

Cleaned up, shaved, with hair combed and cut as best I could manage, I followed the road to the Dresden. I ate frequently, trying to curb my instincts to hunt and kill, and found raw or very rare meat could sustain me, though it never truly satisfied my vast appetite. I had by this time learned some German, and posing as an American tourist, I managed to make my way to West Berlin.

My journey back to America was long and convoluted. By the time I reached New York City by steamship, nearly five years had passed.

I still hungered, but now I chose my victims carefully. They were criminals and cutthroats, murderers and racketeers, the scum of society. I stole everything I wanted from them. When the thirst became too great, I drank their blood—always careful to make it seem as though they had been murdered by rival gangsters. Once, staging the scene of a grisly murder, I paused to wonder how many other such notorious crimes had actually been arranged by my kind. The St. Valentine's Day Massacre? The blood was a giveaway. The Donner Party? Possibly. The Mary Celeste? Rather likely. Any of a hundred more could have been—and probably were—the result of vampire attacks.

And vampire I proclaimed myself. There could be no other answer for my condition. Much as legend, books, and films portrayed us as cold, unfeeling creatures of the grave, the reverse was true. I felt; I needed and yearned and dreamed and hoped and prayed. And I craved companionship. The followers and acolytes I occasionally gathered to myself never proved satisfying. They wanted to *be* like me, to become vampires themselves, but I had no idea how I had become one myself. Biting them didn't seem to do the trick; they remained the same frail, weak creatures they'd always been, and eventually I tired of them and abandoned their kind forever.

In 1960, when I called my parents for the first time since my return from the war, my mother answered the telephone. I was so nervous my hands shook.

"Hello?" she said when nobody answered. "Hello?"

"Mother," I said, "this is Tuck."

There was silence. Then, "If this is your idea of a joke, you're sick." And she hung up.

I called back. The telephone rang, but nobody picked up.

I sat up alone all that night. And the following night I fed on anyone and anything that moved for the first time since Germany. The police blamed a satanic cult. I could have laughed.

I NEVER TRIED to contact my parents again while they were alive, though I dutifully took out a subscription to the weekly *Plainfield Gazette* and began scanning the obituary page. My mother died in 1979, and I came out to see her funeral, standing at the back of her casket lowered into the ground. Mother had always been active in the church. Nearly a hundred people turned out to pay their last respects. It rained; nobody paid any attention to a lone stranger in black who didn't speak and didn't attend the reception afterwards.

And now my father . . .

I had no claim on the family house and lands. Officially I was "lost and presumed dead." I looked perhaps thirty or thirty-five today; nobody would believe me if I came forward and claimed to be sixty-year-old Tucker Anderson, heir to the estate. The farm would probably go to one of our Oakhill relatives.

As I wandered through the house, I realized I wouldn't miss it. Earlier that night, I'd put the executor of my parents' estate to sleep and taken his keys. Alone, I'd driven out, looking for something—though what, I couldn't quite say.

Dishes were stacked two feet high in the kitchen sink, and the cheap formica table had disappeared beneath yellowing newspapers, a scattering of old tools, and the dried-out remains of a dozen TV dinners. I could see where rats or mice had been gnawing at the food and papers.

My parents' bedroom was dirty and unkempt; the bedclothes hadn't been washed in months, probably. There was a sickly sweet smell like infection in the air, so I opened the windows to try and get rid of it.

Then I climbed up the narrow stairs to what had once been the attic, to where my room had been. It felt like I was approaching a gallows.

When I pushed the door open, though, I found my room hadn't changed since I'd left. Clearly nobody had been up here since my mother died, and dust lay like a blankot over everything.

I stood before my bureau, studying the blocky wooden figures I'd carved as a boy. They were crude, not good at all, but they'd occupied my evening hours while listening to The Shadow and Jack Benny on the radio. An old Cardinals baseball card was stuck to the mirror. Gary Lowitt, the name said, but I didn't remember him. Perhaps he was some forgotten hero.

I poked through the bureau drawers, wincing a bit at how worn all my clothes had been. I'd been a ragged kid, pure hick trash. I moved to the closet. The clothes there weren't much better. Most should have been thrown out long before I stopped wearing them.

As I was just about to leave, my gaze fell on a small shoebox peeking out from under a towel on the closet floor. I'd kept my childhood treasures there, I recalled with a sad little smile. How pathetic they must seem now.

Nevertheless, I picked up the box, crossed to the bed, and spilled out the contents. Half remembering, I pawed through Indian arrowheads, bits of string, colored stones, a few Mercury dimes and buffalo nickels, chipped marbles, and half a dozen clippings from old magazines. One article from *Farmer's World* caught my eye, and when I unfolded it, I discovered an ad for a Regulato 155 tractor. The paper's edges felt feathery from being handled so much, and the crease where I'd folded and refolded it had almost cut it in half. I'd loved that tractor as a kid. I'd dreamed of buying Father one for his birthday.

Finally I sighed, scooped my treasures back into their box, added the carvings from my bureau, and only paused to look one last time out the single small, high window. As a kid, I'd always had to stand on a chair to see out. Now it was eye level.

You can come full circle, but you can't go home, I thought sadly. My mother had made that clear the one time I'd called. It was best to let the old ghosts go, to move on and make the best of your life, That was what I'd come here to do, after all, wasn't it?

I ENDED UP staying the night. There were clean sheets in the closet, and I changed my old bed and slept in my old room. Everything and nothing had changed.

If there are such a thing as ghosts, perhaps they touched

me then. When I awakened, the sun streaming in that small window and touching my face, for a second it was 1944 again and I was a kid. I could almost smell bacon frying downstairs, almost hear Father's old tractor puttering away in the yard, almost hear the soft lowing of our cows in the south pasture.

I rose, dressed slowly, and went downstairs to shave and freshen up. In the bathroom, in a little cup on a shelf, sat my father's false teeth. I smiled. He should have seen my teeth, I thought.

As I stared at his, though, it came to me that there was something odd about them, about the way they were cut. The eye teeth seemed too long . . . longer certainly than I remembered, but Father had never been one to smile.

I picked up his teeth and, smiling to show off my fangs, compared both of ours in the mirror. They were identical.

But that's not possible, I thought. How—how could he—.

And then the full horror of it hit me, and I realized what he had been all along. Vampire. Like me. Only he'd never known it.

It wasn't the bite of that German vampire so long ago, I thought, that had infected me with the vampire disease. With a growing sense of horror, I realized I had always been one, only my feeding frenzy—my bloodlust—had never been awakened. If I'd stayed comfortably home on the family farm, I never would have known. I could have lived out my life drowsing away the days like my parents. I might have married and had children of my own, and they too would never have awakened to their true heritage.

I returned to the kitchen table and sank down in one of the faded old chairs. Opening my shoebox of treasures, I stared down at them. For the first time since Germany, I wept.

I had come home at last. I, vampire, son of a vampire, had come full circle.

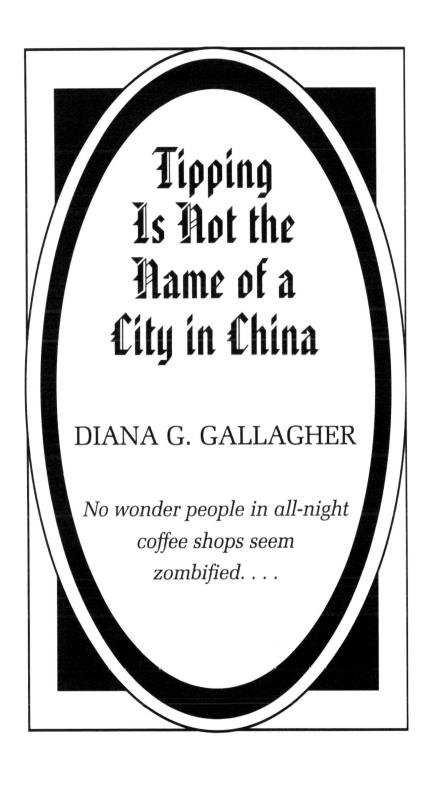

# Tipping Is Not the Name of a City in China

DIANA G. GALLAGHER

*No wonder people in all-night coffee shops seem zombified. . . .*

ORKING GRAVEYARD SHIFT IN A twenty-four hour, motel coffee shop on a remote, desert highway has no advantages—unless one happens to be undead. Being undead doesn't have many advantages, either . . . not for a sun-worshiping, California vegetarian, who likes chocolate and faints at the sight of blood. However, since I was always unrealistically optimistic in life, I see no reason to change now and intend to make the best of it.

Which is why I'm still waiting tables from ten p.m. to six a.m. at the Lucky Clover Cafe on Route 15 about twenty miles southwest of Las Vegas. The physical and emotional transition from human to vampire is not easy, and maintaining a familiar routine is, I suppose, a refuge in denial which is unavoidable during any period of traumatic adjustment.

It's been several weeks since Raven Roberts, lead singer and keyboard player in a top-forty band out of L.A., was booked into the Emerald Isle Casino next door. The band had rooms here, and Raven stopped in for coffee every night after work. Casual conversation eventually led to bed and a sexual affair of such dynamic abandon I still get warm tingles thinking about it. Hopelessly smitten, I slipped him pieces of pie destined to be tossed anyway and routinely forgot to charge him for the coffee, never noticing that neither was ever consumed. He gave me the ultimate tip—eternal undeath. I thought he was kidding.

"Order up!"

Gary Nesmith's gravelly voice isn't just irritating, it's painful. Like many short-order cooks I've worked with, he'd rather be doing something else and, in his case, probably should be. Although he's got the required attitude for the job—I'm the cook (God), you're the waitress (brainless bitch), and the customer (gastronomic idiot) be damned—he's a rotten cook. He's also the owner's brother-in-law and perpetually pissed off because Chance won't put him on swing shift. Even nepotism has its limits.

"What ya waitin' for, Nancy? An engraved invitation? Get your scrawney ass over here before it gets cold!"

I get—not because Gary intimidates me, but because I'm not in the mood to handle dissatisfied customers. However, some diplomacy may be necessary, I realize with a glance at the plate—limp bacon, burned hashbrowns, and runny eggs. Arguing with Gary about the unacceptable condition of the food before someone complains is a waste of time and energy. If it's delivered hot, there's a fifty-fifty chance hungry patrons will ignore greasy bacon and cardboard toast. Tired truckers and travellers are more tolerant at three o'clock in the morning.

Usually.

"Yo! Sweet cheeks!"

I turn back to regard the dirty teamster with wide-eyed innocence, not in the least surprised. "Is something wrong, sir?"

"This ain't my idea of eggs over-hard." He shoves the plate

to the edge of the table.

Coffee pot in hand, I check an impulse to scald him with the steaming, caffeine brew. His crass belligerence raises my cranky-quotient a notch, but he's right.

"I ain't et nothin' in twelve hours, but I'll be damned if I'll eat that shit. Fix it. I get mean when I'm hungry."

A burning sensation surges through my veins, giving new definition to the phrase "mean hunger." I ignore the discomfort and an almost uncontrollable desire to flatten his nose, forcing a broad smile as I take the plate. "Right away. More coffee?"

He starts to nod. Suddenly, his eyes widen and his mouth falls open. Only then am I aware of the pointed, canine teeth slowly descending from my gums.

Closing my own mouth, I retreat to badger Gary into making the trucker another breakfast. Under the best of circumstances, this is difficult. Gary is lazy and considers returned food a personal affront. I can usually diffuse his temper and get a new order with a smile and a few, well-chosen words, either taking the blame for misunderstanding the order or blaming the customer for not having the intelligence to know what he wants. Not this time. My new teeth refuse to retract, and I can't seem to talk without pinching my tongue.

"Ah 'eed 'ese har'." I mumble while keeping my face averted.

"What's your problem?" Gary looks at the plate and sneers. "Ain't nothin' wrong with this. He wanna pay for two meals?"

Fuming, I pull the ticket off the spindle, circle the word HARD (already written in caps), and shove it in his face.

"So? What'dya want me to do about it?"

Nothing, I realize as I follow Gary's gaze to the door. The trucker can't get out of the place fast enough.

"This is comin' outa your pocket, baby. Not mine."

"We'll seeh abou' 'hat." I glare back, then quickly walk away.

I'm famished, but I still haven't resolved the moral dilemma of having to take another life to preserve my own existence . . . not even one as disgusting and useless as Gary Nesmith's. To be honest, the idea of sinking my fangs into somebody's neck and sucking them dry makes me nauseous. So I've put off the inevitable. Bad move.

According to the instructions Raven left behind, (a photocopy of an elegantly handwritten manual that makes me wonder just how long Raven has been a Prince of Darkness and how many sexual consorts he has gratefully converted over the years) it's an issue I'll have to come to terms with soon. Feeding is only necessary every three months or so, but the deadline is upon me, and there's no escape short of volunteering to have a wooden stake driven through my heart or exposing myself to the sun. Neither is an option. Dead or alive, the human will to survive is too deeply ingrained to subvert.

Compounding the basic problem is that if I wait too long, the hunger will take over, and my first meal will be a victim of chance—not choice. The thought of draining the blood from a nice person is more terrifying than the need to kill.

"Who lit the fire under that guy?"

I jump as Chance Ryan storms in, his beady, black eyes blazing. His gaze settles on me when Gary points and sputters.

"She did it, Chance. Musta smart-mouthed that guy or somethin' 'cause he left fightin' mad."

Gary looks more and more appetizing.

Chance, short, fat, balding, and a compulsive gambler who can't resist a long-shot, recognizes a golden opportunity when he sees one. He hits on me—again, slipping a flabby arm around my waist and fixing me with a lascivious leer.

"Nancy, Nancy . . ." A heavy, disappointed sigh is followed by a possessive squeeze. "It's not like you to get uppity with the clientele. I thought you liked this job, but if you're getting so burned out you're chasing away paying customers, I might have to let you go."

Still unable to talk, I hang my head, looking suitably ashamed as I try to wiggle free and fail. Tears, of course, are out of the question. Vampires can't cry. I fake a few sniffles for effect.

"Good God, girl, don't cry!" Chance pulls me into a chest-crushing embrace—not the effect I had in mind. "I'm a reasonable man. We'll talk about it my office after your shift. Okay?"

I nod and step back, snivelling convincingly.

"That's my girl." He grabs my shoulders and frowns. "You're looking kinda pale lately, honey. Get some sun. I liked you much better with a tan. Now—back to work." Grinning, Chance spins me around and pats my rump. I bolt for the ladies room.

It takes five minutes to subdue my rage and coax my fangs back into hiding. Chance has been after my ass since the day I was hired. I'd rather be dead. That thought has an immediate and stunning impact I *am* dead—sort of.

Finally accepting my fate and deciding to give notice, I emerge back onto the floor with a smile. I've had quite enough of the Lucky Clover Cafe, but as Raven's manual cautions, adhering to normal procedures is advisable until such necessities as financial security and a new identity are established. Both will be easily obtained in Las Vegas once I've gotten the hang of certain fringe benefits inherit in my condition—like hypnotic suggestion. I can stake myself working the street without having to service a single trick, buy a new ID, then discreetly hit the casinos for some additional cash.

Nice and neat, but it still leaves me with the original

problem. I'm starving!

However, it's essential to kill and feed without alerting the authorities to anything more unusual than another random murder with no apparent motive, an unofficial, but generally accepted, law of the non-living adopted to minimize obvious complications. Easier done these days than in the past, perhaps. Unfortunately, Raven's Rules Of Conduct strongly advise against satisfying the hunger with acquaintances.

*"Why draw dangerous attention to one's existence?"*

I figure he knows what he's talking about, and I've always been a low-profile, no-risk person anyway. Sleeping with Raven is the most daring thing I've ever done, and look what that got me.

So I've got to find an unsavory stranger—fast—before I embark on my new and exotic unlife as a creature of the night.

As luck would have it, it's mid-week, and traffic into and out of California is light. An hour passes. Not one customer crosses the threshold.

While Gary has made a great show of cleaning the grill and stocking the line for the morning man, Chance has stuffed himself with a steak, two baked potatoes, half a dozen rolls, pie, and coffee. I wait on him, catering to his many demands. In between trips to his table, I make a great show of refilling the salt and pepper shakers and stuffing the sugar caddies— looks like I'm hustling to keep my job and gives me an excuse to stay away from Chance Ryan's prowling hands. (*I* can't charge him with sexual harassment. Appearing in court to testify means daylight and becoming dead for good.)

At last, he rises—no tip—and saunters toward me. His fingers brush my breast as he pauses to remind me of our six a.m. meeting. He winks at Gary on his way out the door.

Obviously, Raven never waited on tables or he'd have

included an exception clause in the "no acquaintances" rule.

By five a.m. I'm beginning to think I should have nailed the trucker. I could have caught him, apologized for my little joke, and made a date to meet him somewhere before dawn. He *was* a jerk . . . with a wife and six kids for all I know.

Sunrise is at 7:11. Checking this vital detail is a habit even novice vampires quickly acquire. I'm running out of time and have to refrain from looking at Gary because every time I do, my fangs begin to drop.

I consider casing the casino for likely prey, then reject that idea, too. All the employees frequent the cafe, They know me. I've never set foot in the Emerald Isle. Going in there now and blatantly trying to get picked-up would raise a few eyebrows and arouse too much curiosity, even if I did just want to get laid. Certainly, I would become the prime suspect when the cops traced a missing person back to the casino—the last place the victim was seen alive.

Instinctively, I know that I cannot postpone quenching my thirst another day and maintain conscious control of my actions. Determined resignation settles over me. The next person that stops for breakfast will be mine.

Wrong.

Chuck Henderson enters, tips his hat, and smiles as he slides into a booth. He's a regular, always pleasant, and a twenty-percent tipper even when he can barely swallow Gary's cooking.

Okay. The next one.

A young woman walks in with a baby in her arms. Her handsome husband follows, leading a toddler by the hand.

I don't think so.

It's five-forty and desperation calls for a re-evaluation of the situation. I am not totally unprepared. Taking Raven's helpful-hints-in-case-of-emergency to heart, I've stashed clothes in a late-model pick-up I purchased a month ago. I traded my old Mustang II and paid the balance in cash. The transaction cleaned out my meager savings and seemed like a foolish extravagance at the time, as did sealing the inside of the camper shell against lethal sunlight. Funny how these things work out. I'll have to ditch the truck before long, of course, but it'll serve my immediate needs.

Gary is watching the clock, anxious to get home to a few beers and a dose of morning cartoons. I smile as I wave good-bye to Chuck and take the young couple's money at the cash register. They leave, and I pocket the night's receipts.

The morning shift is habitually a few minutes late, which suits me just fine today. I stroll to the window overlooking the side parking lot.

"Damn"

"What you bitchin' about now?" Gary shakes his head and rolls his eyes.

"I've got a flat tire."

"Ain't that a shame."

I sigh and look at him helplessly.

"Forget it. I've got better things to do. Call Triple A."

"I'll pay you." I wave a fist full of bills.

Gary walks over, snatches the money from my hand, counts it, and frowns suspiciously. "Thirty bucks? We weren't that busy."

"I always carry extra."

"Yeah, well, lucky for you I'm outa beer and payday's not 'til Friday." He heads for the door.

I dump my tickets on the floor by the open cash register, grab the spare ignition key from my purse, which I leave behind, and hurry after him. No one is in sight outside the casino, and the motel desk clerk has her attention glued to a TV.

Gary circles the truck, then comes to an abrupt halt and whirls to confront me. "What's the deal, bitch? You ain't got no flat—"

Enormous energies flow through me. The look on his face as I bare my fangs, snarl, and knock him out cold will remain one of my fondest memories throughout the centuries to come.

After tossing him into the back of the truck, I climb into the cab, start the engine, and pull around to the office entrance at the rear of the motel. I hesitate, watching Chance through the window, acutely aware that I've already broken Raven's "no acquaintances" rule once. Gary will appease the hunger for weeks, and the incidence of indigestion at the Lucky Clover Cafe will diminish dramatically. Small justification, but I have taken measures to minimize the risks.

The cops will think we were both kidnapped and eliminated as witnesses to a robbery. I'm in the clear. I should just drive away, but if I do, a golden opportunity for sweet vengence spiced with justice will be lost. I'm not the first, poor, working girl my obnoxious employer has tormented with his lecherous passes and roving hands. But I could be the last.

Las Vegas, the gambling capital of the world, is just down the road. I'm smart, immortal, and very hungry. Low-profile, no risk be damned. Sometimes a person has to take a Chance. Gary for breakfast, and the boss for desert. He's not chocolate, but he'll do.

END

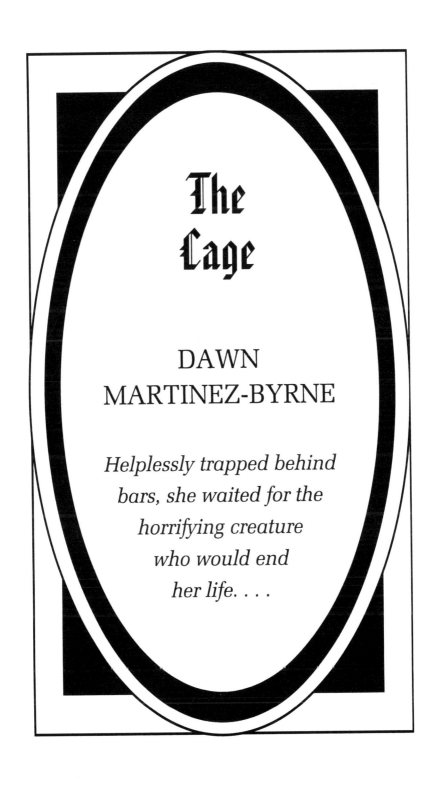

# The Cage

## DAWN MARTINEZ-BYRNE

*Helplessly trapped behind bars, she waited for the horrifying creature who would end her life. . . .*

E KNEW WE WERE IN TROUBLE when Ian got staked.

We were all living in this California city called Riverside. It's not real big, it's not real wild, and it's fairly quiet. Nobody looked for us there. They look for us in Hollywood and LA, and they look in the big houses rich people build on the hills near Laguna and Malibu. But they never look in places like Riverside.

Al found it for us. Al's real name is Alessandro, but I call him Al. We've been together for a while now. He found me when I was hanging out with Georges LaFleur in San Francisco. Al thought I was way too young to be with Georges. But all Georges said was "Tasha, she outbite us all. You know?" Al said he knew and he didn't care, I was too young and he wanted me to come with him. That was when I knew I wanted to be with Al. Nobody ever cared what I did before.

We moved around and finally came to Riverside. We had a security apartment and stayed quiet. We hunted together and met up with some others from around here. Ian was pretty flamboyant; he rode around in a big limo and had all these gold rings he made people kiss when they got into his car. He'd make his driver go around and around while he fed in the back. He had this list of all the vampires in the area and whenever he had a party he called us. Al didn't really like him; he said Ian was going to get us all staked if he didn't settle down. Ian didn't listen. Now he was staked.

We saw it in the paper: a little article about a weird murder in Canyon Crest, the posh area of Riverside. Alessandro made me read it out loud to him five or six times. He wanted the hunter, because this guy was a pro. Ian was staked, and then his head was cut off and his mouth filled with garlic. If he'd just been staked, then maybe Alessandro could have helped revive him. But with the head cut off, and the mouth stuffed with garlic, it's all over. The police were looking for the murderer. Now so were we.

We heard more about Ian from Jamey. He called and warned us that Ian's list had disappeared, and that we'd better move. Jamey showed up with some friends to help us. He was like a lot of us, quiet and respectable. He worked at a blood bank, getting us the bottled stuff that the doctors couldn't use. Alessandro mixed it with some other things so it'd be potent enough for us to drink. That way we weren't hunting all the time and drawing attention to ourselves. You'd never take any of us for vampires. And I think that's why I was so shocked at Ian. He was flashy, but he was also careful. He didn't take anyone that might get missed. He knew where the people are who no one misses, and he always took them for rides.

After we loaded Jamey's van we went inside to talk. He had an idea, and he wanted us to hear it.

Al locked the door and closed the drapes. "Tell us what you think."

"Why don't we use Tasha as bait?"

DAWN MARTINEZ-BYRNE

"What?" I yelled.

"Listen. It'll work. You work at that arcade, right?"

I worked at the Castle. You know, the place right off the freeway, Arcade and Golf, family FUN FUN FUN! That place. The arcade is made like a Castle, with a big, bright garish miniature golf course. "Yeah, I work there."

"What would you have her do?" demanded Alessandro.

"They have a change booth, right near the pool tables. See if you can get them to let you work that. That way, we can be all over the arcade watching you, and he can't get at you. See?"

Al looked at the floor for several seconds. "We would all have to be there, to stop him if he should appear."

"That's right. Then we can deal with him."

"What if he gets me?" I asked.

"I have a bulletproof vest you can use," said Jamey. "He can't stake you."

"He cannot harm you," said Al "We will be there."

I knew that tone. It was decided. "OK," I said.

I HAD to trade with another girl so I'd get the Change Booth. This was the best arcade I'd worked in, and I'd worked in a lot of them. They took care of the games here. If you're the gambling type you could play Skeeball or Boomball or Twenty-One and save the little tickets for prizes. Most people cashed them in right away for little bits of junk, but some hung on to them and waited until they had ten or twenty thousand and then cashed them in all at once. There was a color TV for 25,000 points once, and I'm glad I didn't work when it went. Each one of those damn tickets has to be counted by the prize person, and then the big things have to be listed in a log. And then you have to go and get the stuff. The TV was in a glass case right next to the prize counter, so that wasn't too bad, but some of that stuff is buried. I liked prizes the best. Some of the toys were fun to play with when there was nothing else to do. I'd never worked the change booth before, but I knew it couldn't be too bad.

I WAS worried about the hunter all day. We fed on bottles before we left so we wouldn't get weak. Sometimes they shut real late on Saturday. That could give this hunter all the time he'd need. Al wanted that. He sometimes hung out with me at the Castle, so nobody'd care if he played the rifle shoot game or some other quick win game all night. And he might spot the hunter and take care of him. There's a lot of dark corners on the golf courses.

It was already dark when we got there. I went into the break room to put away the vest, then hung around the clock until it was time to punch in. Terry came in while I was waiting, whistling and swinging his catcher's mitt. I like Terry. He's a nice, smart guy, majoring in business. I think he kind of knew about me and Al but he never mentioned it. He kind of hinted, but that's all. I think he thought we were cool.

Ron the manager came in. "Ready, Tasha?"

"Yeah."

"Have fun in the Cage," said Terry.

Ron led me out to the booth. It was bright blue and white, with this flashing yellow sign that said CHANGE. It only had a half door, so you had to get down and crawl in. He unlocked it and let me in, then handed me the cash drawer and a bag full of change. "Have fun," he said, and locked the door.

I saw why Terry called it the Cage. It was just barely large enough for me to sit in it and still be comfortable. There was a drawer with a notepad in it, a couple of pencils, and room to stick money. Overhead was an old-fashioned lamp, with three big white globes, and a fan. I flipped the switch and the lights and fan came on. A nice breeze filled the little room, cool and relaxing after the breathless June day.

I was glad I was in here, where it was cool and safe. Golf would be miserable, because there's open windows to the course and the hunter would have a clear shot at me. And every kid for miles around would be playing golf tonight. Prizes would be bad, too, because this was the kind of night where people decide it's time to trade in ten thousand one point Skeeball tickets ten minutes before you shut. I pitied the girls in the snack bar. The line was already long and on Saturday night it doesn't go away until we're closed, usually around one or so in the morning. I hated the snack bar. Orders get screwed up, both because the airhead taking the order isn't paying attention and because the customers change their minds four or five times and then get mad when you don't know what they want. Then there's people who want exotic things, like the veggie burgers or veggie dogs with veggie chili and cheese. And of course the snack bar gets hot, and the longer the shift, the hotter it gets. I was nice and cool in the Cage.

I pulled the rolls of dimes and quarters and started filling the dispensers. They looked like mutant microscopes. They give you fifty cents a pull, so you have to hit them twice for a buck. That confuses some people. After I loaded them I filled up the roll holder that's built right into the Cage. I unscrewed the little thing that blocks the change hole and I was in business.

Customers weren't overwhelming me and it didn't look like I'd see too much traffic. Some kids started playing Cosmic Guerilla, the huge video game right next to the Cage. The thick brown carpet that lined the bottom of the Cage absorbed the noise of the arcade, making my cocoon even more enjoyable. I fished the notepad out and began drawing pictures. You're supposed to write orders for cash on it, but so what. I had a lot on my mind. Maybe no one would come. That wouldn't break my heart. I'd get to sit in the nice cool Cage for six hours and think.

"Quarters," said a man.

I looked up. A man waved a dollar and pushed it through the cash door. The breeze from the fan caught the dollar and pulled it in.

"How did you do that?" he asked. "I've got a fan in here."

He couldn't hear me. The little screen that they talked through was higher than I sat, and anyway he'd never hear me over the screaming and shooting from Cosmic Guerilla. "I have a fan."

"I don't have a van," he said.

"Never mind," I said as loudly as was polite. I pulled the lever on the dispenser and counted how many quarters I got. It's supposed to give out two, but every now and then it screws up and gives out three. The dime ones like to screw up too and give out six dimes instead of five. I gave the man his quarters and he left.

I went back to my picture. Cosmic Guerrilla makes this awful electronic beeping that gets worse as the game progresses. There were a couple of little kids playing it, screaming and yelling while it wore them down. I could see Al in the distance, his cloak draped over the corner of a pinball game. He wanted his cloak with him. It's been his for so long that he won't part with it. I can see that. It's a nice cape. It's really not what you'd think of us having at all. It's burgundy velvet, with all these gold patterns on it. It was his back when he lived in Spain, so it's old. And if the guy who staked Ian busted in and trashed our place, he wanted it safe.

He doesn't talk much about what he was before. His real name is long and then there's all these other names behind it.

They were like a pedigree or something. I know he was a conquistador, and that he was in Mexico. That's where he got changed. He said that he was in service to a very powerful old Cardinal who's even stronger than a vampire. He said he was damned to a life of purgatory, but never excommunicated. The way he said it was so painful I never asked him anything else. I guess he's what he is because of what he was, but he doesn't talk about it very much.

I couldn't see what game he was playing, but that didn't matter. They're all good. I'd rather play pinball than the dumb video games. Pinball requires skill. Al feels the same way. That's why we're a good match. We're both kind of old-fashioned traditionalists.

I didn't really fit in with Georges. He was kind of a playboy, with girls and drugs and blood everywhere. His whole place was red with black floors and ceilings. Someone had run a bunch of little lights all over the ceilings so it would look like the sky. There were speakers in every room, and he'd broadcast the sounds of whatever orgy he was having all through the place. And then there were the drugs. I think the drugs were for the people who came in to see him, cause they don't do anything for me and I don't see how they'd do anything for any of us.

I was eighteen when I left home to Find Myself. I wasn't getting married and I wasn't going to college. My parents didn't care what I did, just as long as I didn't embarrass them in front of their friends at the club. So I went to Napa, and that's where I met Georges. He had it all and I went right along with him. I don't think it was even a month before I was a vampire.

A dollar blew into me. I caught it before it hit the floor. "I want some tens," said a little voice. I looked up, then over the edge of the counter. There was a little tiny girl, no more than five, clutching a fistful of dollar bills. Her hair was braided into little cornrolls and she had eye makeup on. I gave her the dimes and she walked away. A lot of people use the Castle as a baby-sitter, especially around Christmas. I watched her go and dump all her money on one of the Skeeballs and start to play.

Seeing that little girl really pissed me off. She could get into all kinds of trouble here alone. What were her folks doing? She shouldn't have been here alone at night like this. Somebody could rip off her money, or worse. This little kid wasn't even ten. Her parents didn't deserve her. She'd end up with a guy like Ian or Georges and they'd piss and moan that their baby was gone. It was their own damn fault. I can't take people like that. My mom was like that. They shouldn't have kids if they're going to just dump them off wherever the hell is convenient for them.

If I hadn't been worried about the hunter, I might have pointed her out to Al. That way he could locate her folks, and later we could drop in on them. I'd just do it once, cause after that it never has the same effect. I wanted them to see what could happen to their kid, if they even cared about her at all.

A giant biker with leathers on came up to the booth. This guy was huge, even taller than Al! He had the Harley colors flying proud on his chest. I waited for him to pick up the Cage like it was a piggybank and shake it until all the money came cascading out. Where was Al? He'd get rid of this guy.

He bent over and looked in the screen. I knew I was dead.

"Excuse me, miss," he said softly, "may I have a roll of quarters?"

"Huh?"

He put down two fives. "Quarters?"

"Yeah, sure. OK." I handed him the orange paper tube.

"Thank you," he said, and walked away.

Why couldn't that little kid have this guy for a dad?

But I should know better than to go judging by looks. Some of the ones who hung around Georges were gorgeous and real bastards. I was afraid of most of them. The night Alessandro came I had to sit around in this leather strap and chain thing that exposed my boobs. I was supposed to be one of Georges' sex pets. I felt like an idiot in that thing and when Al said I was too young to be there I wanted to die.

He said he'd been sent by the Cardinal to warn Georges that his behavior was too obvious and that he was running the risk of exposure. Georges laughed at him and called him the Cardinal's enforcer and *La Sombra de la Muerte*, the Shadow of Death. Al told Georges to release me and to settle down before the Cardinal took action. Georges snickered, but he did let me take my things out. I moved in with Alessandro in this house near the Marina. It was full of antiques and guns and all kinds of old stuff. I got used to being treated well in a hurry.

Nothing was happening, so I started watching the pool games down in the Dungeon. The Cage was almost all glass on top, so it was a great vantage point. You could see the whole Dungeon and most of the arcade. There's a different rate for the pool games, depending on how many are playing. It's fairly common for people to say they have two players and really have five or so on a table. There were some gangbangers down there, and then I saw Jamey and a couple of others playing on Table 5. At least they were here, where they could see me.

One night, when Al was out in the car waiting for me, some gangbangers decided to start a fight. They stabbed one guy and bashed his Monte Carlo all to hell. The security guards busted it up fast, but not before the gangbangers ran over a guy and shot someone else. Al went and grabbed one of them when he tried to run away. He fed off that guy and left him in the bushes for security to find. I was sorry I missed out.

A big, hulking cowboy came up and shoved a twenty in at me. "What do you want?" I asked.

He glared at me. I expected him to spit tobacco juice all over the kids playing Cosmic Guerilla. "Quarters. Many as you got."

I handed him two rolls of quarters and put the bill away.

"I gave you a twenty," he said.

"I know," I yelled. "That's twenty dollars in quarters. Rolls are ten each."

He stared at me for a minute. "I know." He picked up the brown and orange tubes and swaggered off.

I checked the clock over the pool tables. 8 PM. The Castle was pretty full now. I could see the banks of Twenty-Ones. They're kind of a barometer for the arcade. When they fill up, you're in for a busy night. They were full now, and people were milling around behind them, waiting for the players to relinquish their machines. It never occurred to them to go and play other things, but then, some of the games at the Castle are pretty hard. Twenty-One requires that you be able to put a dime or a quarter in a slot and roll a ball. For a lot of the customers those requirements are almost more than they can handle.

But people are like that. They never think for themselves. They see *Dracula* on TV and then they go looking for us to stake. I wished Ian hadn't been so damn neat and tidy, with his big address book all fixed out for the hunter to go looking through.

This tall guy with a beaky nose left a Twenty-One and came to me. He was a born leader, because suddenly all these people left Twenty-Ones and got in line behind him. They were just like cows. People never think.

He pushed five dollars in and I grabbed them before they blew away. "Quarters," he said, smiling. "Hurry up. My wife is waiting."

I nodded and started counting coins.

"She's waiting," he said.

"How long have you been married?" I asked, like I cared.

"Since this morning. She and I want to spend the night here. So long."

That stopped me. This was a new one. I looked over at the Twenty-Ones. There she was, all decked out in a fluffy wedding gown. Al was a few customers back. I wanted him to see this, so I pointed at the Twenty-Ones. Everyone turned to look, and when they saw the Bride of the Castle some of them started laughing. A couple of guys whistled and someone clapped.

Al gave me some bills and I handed him his quarters. He spent a few minutes looking in at me. I love the way he looks at me like he wants to consume me. I love that look. I think that was what made me like him, that and the fact that he made all of Georges' creeps leave me alone. I could have looked at him all night. But the line was way long and he had to move on. He wandered over to the Twenty-Ones. Some kid saw him and ran away from his machine, so Al sat down and started playing.

Money blew in, coins went out. Dollar in dimes, roll of quarters, five dimes, two in quarters, three in quarts, one in quarters. I had the feel for it now, so I stopped thinking about what I was doing and started thinking about what we were going to do tonight.

I'd do anything to keep Alessandro safe. Not that he needs it, but I'd do it anyway. When he made Georges hand me over I felt so relieved I swore I'd kill anyone who hurt him. That's kind of funny because I'm nowhere near as strong as he is.

And now there was the hunter. Who was I looking for, anyway? I didn't know this guy. What was I supposed to look for? Someone who came up a lot, or just once? Some guy with crosses and garlic breath or someone real quiet and reserved? I couldn't tell this guy from any normal customer. I was trapped in here, where he could see me, and I had no idea who he was.

I wanted out of that Cage. I wanted to be out in the night with Al. I wanted to fly past and stay away from the regular people. I wanted to be free.

*Free* was one of the things Georges used to get me. That and never getting old. When you're 18 you hope you have forever. You hope that the world is going to stop for you, and that you won't ever get old or sick or die. It'd always happen to someone else. I sure felt that way, and when Georges said that if I did a couple little things I'd be free of it, I jumped. I didn't know what I was doing, and I didn't care.

Once I got settled in, I knew that everyone I ever met was going to be gone and I'd keep going. I never figured out why people said we were dead, though. It's not like dead. Dead is the cat you ran over with the car. Dead is the guy who got shot by some idiot kid. We're not dead. We live, we make love we move. Dead doesn't move.

What was the poem I liked, Death be not Proud. The only time I think about death is when some little kid gets killed. Then you realize how much life you need to have life. That's what makes us different. Everyone's a vampire, in one way or another. Whether you live off of plants or off of blood, it's the same thing. You need life for life.

Smoke blew into the Cage. That got my attention. A kid in a Pearl Jam T-shirt handed me a five and took a long drag off his cigarette. You're not supposed to smoke in here. It stung for a few seconds and bothered me for a long time afterwards. I gave him his damn quarters and called security to report him.

The next few dozen people went pretty fast. I tried not to think about why I was sitting there. The line was moving pretty

DAWN MARTINEZ-BYRNE

good, and I could even see Alessandro now and then, scaring kids away from machines he wanted to play. I saw the clock go to 10, then 10:30. Things were going good.

A tall hardfaced woman with curly hair and a bunch of cheap gold cross necklaces pushed forward. I didn't like her. For a minute I thought she might be the hunter. She looked like the type that would run roughshod over whatever the hell got in her way. A twenty came in to me. "I want a ten, a five, four ones and four quarters," she said through her nose.

I hate it when people say things like that. I don't know how else I'm supposed to break twenty and give them a buck in quarters, unless maybe I give them quarters and a nineteen or something. I started counting bills. There were some brand new ones, and they were sticking together.

She didn't want to wait. "Are you trying to cheat me?" she screeched. I shoved her change at her and she left.

She reminded me of something wild that happened when we were living in San Jose. These Born Agains came to the door with this giant cross and all these pamphlets about Jesus. It was getting dark and Al and I had just gotten up. And here were these women singing at us about Jesus. I don't know what they said, but all of a sudden Al lost it.

He grabbed the cross and it burst into flames. The women started screaming and Al yelled back at them in Spanish. I don't know what he was saying, but the Mexican guy next door crashed his lawnmower into a bush and ran away screaming. Al kept it up and the pamphlets burst into flames and then they started spitting blood everywhere. The cross was spitting blood too and the women were getting covered with bits of boiling blood. They backed up and Al went after them, yelling and waving the cross around. They piled into their car and he slammed the cross down on the trunk. It burned a huge black cross right into the metal. The cross spit up blood and flames and the women were screaming and crying and trying to get away. They finally got the car to go and they took off so fast they went over the curb and gouged marks in the road where they hit.

Al made us pack up and leave there that night. It was a good thing, too, because the Born Agains came back while we were moving. We had already taken one load of things away and were coming back for the rest when we saw these people standing in the driveway. There was a preacher there, holding a Bible and shouting all sorts of stuff at the house. Al got mad, and said that a bunch of Heretics weren't going to exorcise him from the house. He wanted to go and get rid of all of the Heretics. That's what he called them. Heretics. I was scared. There were so many of them, and only two of us. We had already taken the important things. The stuff left in the house was junk that we could replace. It wasn't worth getting them all excited and maybe staking us. He finally decided to do it my way and we drove past. But he couldn't resist opening the window and saying something in Spanish. The last we saw of them, the preacher was on his knees screaming and the cross was spitting blood.

Some guy tapped at the glass. "Change?"

That brought me back. "Yeah. OK. I can handle that." I gave him his money and he left.

I had to watch it. What if he'd been the hunter? I couldn't afford to drift away like that again.

It was 11 and the freak show was in full swing. There were more people in the Castle than I had ever seen before. People could have dropped dead out there and they would have never hit the floor. That crowd would have just kept right on pushing them along. I shoved five hundred dollars into a bag and called

DAWN MARTINEZ-BYRNE

Ron out to the Cage to take it. I was almost out of dimes and I had less than a roll of quarters left. I looked at the line of customers. Maybe I could placate a few of them.

"Quarrrrrs," said the first man as he tried to put a dollar in the window. He was way past the point of knowing where he was. I gave him the quarters and he stumbled away.

A bunch of little kids crushed forward. They dumped a torn brown bag full of pennies, nickels and ones out on the counter. I scooped the mess in and began to count. "What do you guys want?"

They thought for a minute, then changed tactics and started fighting. I gave them a couple dollars in quarters and the rest in dimes. They were silent for a whole second while they looked at what I gave them, and then they started fighting over who got what and how many.

A big burly man with tattoos over every square inch of his arms shoved the kids out of the way. They retreated a few steps and then began yelling at him. He threw a five at me. "Roll of dimes."

Fortunately I had a single roll of dimes left. I handed it to him and he turned to go. Just then one of the little kids darted in front of him and he tripped. The roll of dimes dropped from his fist and burst open.

The kids shrieked and dove for the dimes. People started picking them up. He was shouting and screaming threats at everything that moved. The kids disappeared into the crowd and the man was left with half a roll of dimes. He saw me laughing at him and started yelling at me through the side glass. While he was screaming I tried to help other people, but the next guy wanted a roll of dimes and the last on I'd had was now scattered throughout the arcade. I apologized and we all waited.

45

The burly man pushed that poor guy aside and crammed his face against the glass. "You goddamn bitch," he roared, "I've had it with you ripping me off. I want the manager of this joint out here so I can see him!"

Damn, I wanted Al there. This bastard needed Al!

"You hear me?" he screamed, and tried to reach through the opening. "I want the manager now!"

Where the hell was Al when I needed him?

"You wanted to see me?" asked Ron.

The big man peeled away from the cage. Ron shoved the money bag in to me and took the man away.

I handed the next guy his dimes and went back to dealing with the line. Pretty soon I had my old rhythm back: buck in quarters, two in dimes. The line was flying. I looked around to see if I recognized any of the customers. I didn't. I didn't see Alessandro anywhere, either. I wanted him where I could see him.

A woman with a little boy handed me a five and two ones. She glared coldly at me and said, "I want three ones and four dollars worth of dimes."

This made no sense. "Excuse me, but why did you give me the two ones when you wanted three back? Why didn't you just hand me the five?"

She stared at me like I'd just suggested she pose nude on top of Cosmic Guerilla. "What?" she snapped. "I didn't intend to bother you!" She grabbed her boy by the hair and yanked him away.

It was quiet for a few minutes. I couldn't see Al anywhere. Now I was worried. What if he'd run into the hunter? I turned to see if Jamey was around, but they had quit playing pool. I was alone.

I never felt so helpless before. Never. I was in a glass box and there was no one around I could yell to. I mean, I could use the phone, but it only called the prize counter. I felt sick at being so damn vulnerable.

Some girls came up. They work at the Castle, but they aren't employed by the Castle. They are there every night, working. I doubt if there's a male regular at the Castle they don't know by more than name.

They were a lot like the girls that used to hang out at Georges'. They were pretty in a hard way, with no heart left in them because it had all been drained away. Georges always used them cause he'd have them pick these guys up and we'd all get to feed off of them. Georges almost never kept the guys around. Usually he had them burned, so they wouldn't come back. Once in a while he kept one alive but that was only if they were going to be useful to him. The ones he kept were creepy and mean.

The last time I saw Georges was a few nights after Alessandro took me away. We had already moved my things and now we were supposed to go to a party at Georges to say good-bye. Georges was mad. He kept yelling at Al who ignored him. He tried to make me stay, but I wanted out. And then he went and shoved a cross at Al.

Alessandro got mad. He said something in Spanish and shoved it away. He told Georges he'd made his decision. He made me get into a car and we drove to our new place.

A couple days later Al took me over to a building near Georges'. We could see his place just fine. All of a sudden the whole place just exploded in flames. Not normal flames, but this weird blue-green fire. I could feel them screaming in their rooms and coffins. It wasn't a sound, it was a sense. I clung to Al and he hid me under his velvet cloak. I hung on to him for a long time, until the last of the howls faded away and sirens screamed the arrival of the fire department.

I am lucky to be with him. I don't know if he set Georges up, or if he was there to warn Georges that it was about to be set up. I don't care. Al said only that it was a bad idea to anger the Cardinal, and I left it alone.

I tried to concentrate back on the Castle. I wanted out of the Cage. More easy requests. My line was way shorter now. I saw the same people come through the line. Maybe one of them was the hunter. I couldn't tell from in here, and I couldn't see any of my protectors. The arcade was still busy, but it had died way back. The Twenty-Ones were starting to empty and stay that way. I could even see the prize counter. Terry was there, handing out little plastic dinosaurs to the kids with the guy's dimes. One of the other prize people stabbed him with a 15 point plastic dagger and they kept horsing around.

Alessandro wandered up. "Hi lover," he said through the little screen.

I was so glad to see him I wanted to shout. "Where've you been?"

"Wandering. Jamey is out on the golf course."

"OK. What about everyone else?"

"They are in the parking lot."

"OK. I should be done soon."

He smiled and gave me that hungry look. "Yes."

"Any sign of that hunter guy?"

The smile went. Gone. "No." He turned and walked away.

There was no one else in line. Snack bar was closing down; they had the popcorn machine shut off and cleaned, and they were working on shutting off ice cream, too.

There were only a couple of Twenty-Ones busy. No one was on Cosmic Guerilla. I saw the last of the pool players turn in the balls and the Dungeon was quiet. Ron picked up the mike at the Prize counter and announced that the Castle would be closing in ten minutes. He called me on the phone and said to shut down.

That was the best thing I'd heard all night. I screwed the little hole cover back in and started re-rolling the dimes from the dispenser. The burly man with all the tatoos stalked over to the prize counter. As long as he stayed away from me I didn't care what he did. I should have had Al deal with him. I finished the dimes and started on the quarters.

"Lover," said Al through the screen. "I'm going to go out now. I'll wait for you."

"What time is it?"

He looked over at the clock. "One fifty-three."

No wonder I was shot. "Fine. I'll see you."

He turned and walked out, slinging his cloak across his shoulders as he left.

Ron picked up the mike again. The Castle was closed. I shoved the rolls back into the bag and waited for him to rescue me.

The arcade power shut off with a weird electric scream. Ron directed the big man out the door to the catapult gate. He still hadn't come, so I started to straighten out the ones, fives, tens and twenties in the drawer. I was still counting when the big man ran back in.

"The damn gate's locked and there's a *vampire* walking around out there!"

Everybody laughed at him. Terry pointed at me, still in the Cage. "That's her boyfriend. He won't hurt you."

"The hell he won't. I ain't going out the gate where that sucker is. No way."

Ron called one of the guards to come and let the guy out. They escorted him over to one of the big doors. "Sonovabitching vampire, that's what he is," said the man.

"Don't forget your cross!" the guard yelled after him.

Ron came and let me out. He and the guards were still laughing, screaming "I vant to bite your neck!" I laughed at them.

I clocked out and went into the restroom to put on the bulletproof vest. It was big, but so what. I zipped up my uniform and headed out the catapult gate. No one was there. That was weird, because usually Alessandro waited for me there. He was gone. The other girls had already left, so I couldn't walk out to the car with a bunch of them. They made us park over by the dumpsters. Usually I didn't care, but not tonight. Now all I could see were a few cars away across the lot.

I didn't screw around. I ran. I ran over the pavement, scattering gravel. I slammed full tilt into the car on the end and waited. No one was around. I could see the police helicopter spiralling around, sweeping its light over the buildings across from the Castle. I wished they were looking for the hunter. I fished out my keys and carefully started for the car.

The dumpster smelled bad. I couldn't see anything. I slid over and reached for the car door. Something flew over my head and went tight at my throat. I reached up and tried to pull it off, but it burned into my hands. I fell onto the car and my hands were grabbed and pulled behind me.

"Vampire bitch!" screamed a man. "You're going to die tonight!"

I tried to get up, but he yanked the rope and I fell on my face. He slammed a knee in my back and started screaming about God and Hell. The rope burned, like someone was holding hot wires around my hands and throat. I tried to get free, but he twisted the rope tighter.

Where was Al? I needed him now!

He grabbed me by my hair and hauled me out into the parking lot. I tried to break away, but when I did the burning got worse. He shoved me down on my knees and dropped a backpack on the ground.

I looked up at him. He was a thickset, beefy man with red hair and a huge cross. He had a metal collar around his neck. When he saw me looking at him, he shoved the cross in my face. I had to pull away. He held it there and forced me onto my back. I saw him pull something out of the backpack. It was a crossbow, loaded with a stake.

He pulled the rope until I was down flat. It hurt to move. The pain was so bad I felt like he was cutting through my skin. He grabbed the front of my uniform and zipped it open. When he saw the vest, he started laughing. "You can't stop me!" he screamed. "I know your tricks! You can't fool me!" And he tore it and my bra away from me.

I knew I was dead. He stood over me, shoving the tip of the stake next to my breast and right over my heart. I almost wished he'd do it, so I wouldn't hurt so bad.

"Alessandro!" he shouted. "Come to me! I have her and I will kill her! Come to me! My vengeance is now!"

I was crying then, from fear and pain. I wanted Al to save me, but I didn't want him to be killed. I felt like I was being burned away, drowned in blinding light. "No!" screamed the hunter.

I looked up. We were surrounded by cop cars, their lights focused on the hunter. The helicopter was right over us too, its light shining down. *"Drop your weapon now!"* ordered a voice.

THE COPS made us fill out a bunch of forms. They kept look-ing at the burns on my neck and hands. They wanted me to go to the hospital but Alessandro told them he'd take me to our family doctor in the morning. I knew that meant he'd take care of me himself.

I had Al's cloak over my shoulders, so I was covered. I leaned on him while the cops dealt with the hunter. They had him in handcuffs. Spread out on the pavement was all his junk from the backpack. I couldn't see everything he had in it, but I could see the stakes. Alessandro kept me close while they took pictures of everything. The cops finally pushed the guy into the back of one of their cars. Overhead the helicopter spun away, trailing its light through the trees.

I wanted to get this guy stopped. "Is this the guy who killed that man in Canyon Crest?"

"We'll be investigating that," said the cop taking my statement.

"I hope he fries." I said.

The cop looked at me. "He won't be going anywhere for a while. There's a number of things we want to discuss with him."

"It is good that he will be put away." said Al "Thank you for your time, officer. We will be leaving the area anyway."

"I hate to see that," said the cop, "but I understand."

We watched the cops break away before going to Al's car. The red haired hunter saw us and flipped out. I saw him struggling in the back of the car, trying to bust loose. He started screaming, "Vampires! They're vampires! You have to free me! I have to stop them! They're *vampires!*"

Some of the cops laughed. Most didn't. We drove past them, the man's yelling echoing through the night like the screech of an owl.

When we were clear of them I started crying. "Why didn't you come and get me? Why did you let him hurt me?"

Alessandro stopped the car. I could see he was crying, too. "Because," he said finally, "I knew that as long as I was away, you would be safe. I had Jamey call the police. It was the only way I could keep you."

I collapsed on him and hung on for a long time.

So now we move on. Alessandro says San Antonio is nice. Maybe we'll try there. Like they say, we're eternal.

# Runaway

## DARRELL
## SCHWEITZER

*Some horrors
children encounter
are worse than
others.*

Y THE TIME he picked me up, I might have been standing by the side of that highway for hours. I couldn't remember much, just then, only the darkness and the rain and the soft, soothing sound of the traffic, and how I was very tired and something hurt but I didn't know quite what.

He was honking his horn. "Hey kid! You coming?"

I ran for the car, clutching my knapsack tightly against my chest. Then we were moving, and I felt sleepy, but he was one of the ones who want to talk.

"Where you going?"

"Just going."

"I see. But you'll know where it is when you get there."

"I guess so."

I held the knapsack in my lap, and I brought my knees up, feet on the seat, gripped my knees, and leaned my face against the window, watching the landscape roll by, black and gray and flashes of light that seemed to streak and bob and slowly drift down the wet glass.

"Jesus, it's no night for you to be out," he said. "Skinny kid like you, in just that light jacket and jeans and sneakers. You haven't even got any socks. You must be soaked to the skin. You'll catch your death—"

"I'm not cold. I don't feel it."

He reached over and touched me on the leg. "You're frozen like ice! Christ!"

"I'm okay."

"What *you* need is a good hot meal; a hot shower; and new, warm clothes; and maybe a friend who can provide all those things."

I just turned away, let my feet drop to the floor, and stared out the side window. I was crying softly. I didn't know why. The sound of the wheels on the pavement was like a soft voice far away, singing, and the rain had turned into sleet and it clattered on the roof. I watched the farmhouses pass, one by one, vanishing into the darkness, and the people inside them were like warm points of light, like candle flames, far away, but definitely there, alive. Then gone. I listened to the night, while the man in the car with me chattered on and on, about how this sure was big, beautiful country we had here in the Midwest—but was I from around here? I didn't sound like it. He was from California, which was beautiful too; but, hey, see America first, even if the only vacation he could get was in October; autumn in the mountains of Tennessee and Virginia, the leaves turning color, quite a sight—

I started to remember things, and I was afraid, and the tears came more freely.

He was silent for a while.

Finally he said, "My name is Howard."

The traffic went by, the sleet and rain beat down, and the night was dark.

"You must have a name," he said.

DARRELL SCHWEITZER

"Lawrence."

"Larry, then. Do your friends call you Larry?"

"I suppose so."

More silence. He kept looking at me, sideways as he drove, sizing me up, as if he were, it seemed to me, not just a friend, not just someone who felt sorry for me and wanted to help, but someone who was—I couldn't put it any other way—hungry.

"Are you running away from home, Larry?"

"Leaving."

"How old are you, Larry?"

"Uh . . . fifteen."

"At your age, do you think it's such a good idea to be out on your own? Not that I want to sound like a parent. I mean, I respect a young man who is independent and can decide things for himself—"

The memories came flooding back now, all the pain.

"It's because of my mom."

"She's a real bitch then? Women are like that. Real bitches sometimes. You have to get away." He launched into another long monologue about mothers and wives and such. I wasn't listening. Up ahead, lights flashed. Traffic slowed down. We sat still for several minutes, then crept forward, then sat again, until a policeman in a yellow raincoat waved us onto the shoulder and around two smashed cars and a jack-knifed truck; cops and people everywhere, ambulance lights whirling.

"Looks bad," Howard said.

The warmth. The burning lights, like candles flickering, going out. There was death here.

"Looks real bad," Howard said. "Somebody could have been killed."

"Two. Two dead. Another will die soon."

He looked at me funny and shook his head. "Oh."

Then we drove in silence for a while, and I reached into my knapsack and touched. I tried to hold back tears a third time, but couldn't. I was so ashamed.

"You said it was your mom," Howard said. "Maybe it will help if you tell me. Get it all out. She was a domineering bitch. Beat you, did she? I bet she drove your dad right out of the house."

"Actually, she killed him. Then she sold her soul to the Devil."

The car lurched. *"What?"*

I smiled inwardly, bitterly. I could have been making all this up, and he would still have to listen, because of the hurt he might do me if it were all true and he said he didn't believe me . . . like those Jews the Nazis tortured and stuff, you can't say they're lying, not to their faces, because if they really *were* there and it really *did* happen . . .

"Mom used to put black candles in my room at night," I said, "and make drawings on the floor and walls, stars and circles and things like that she called *sigils.* My dad said it was all bullshit, but Mom said that if you really want to get something, there are things you just have to do. They fought a lot, yeah. He beat her up till her face was all bloody. I remember the time he smashed her head into the TV screen and the glass cracked. Fortunately the TV was off at the time. So she killed him."

"Right then?"

"No, later."

"Can you blame her?"

"No. Not really."

He was following along now. I might have been remembering; but, for all he knew, I might have been making up a story. Either way, I had him *caught.* It felt good. He was getting real nervous, pounding his hands on the steering wheel, looking at me, then back at the road, then at me again, breathing hard.

"Don't you think . . .? I mean, the police . . ."

"No."

"Why . . .?"

"My mom was a witch. Maybe that's why Dad hated her. Maybe she became a witch because he hated her first. I don't know."

"That's a very perceptive thing for someone . . . who's been through what you have . . . to say."

"Oh," I shrugged and stared out the window for a while, remembering or dreaming.

"Oh Christ," he said to himself in a low, whiny voice over and over. "Oh Christ, why did I have to get this one? Oh Christ . . ."

"Mom's friends were witches too," I said, "or at least they were after a while. She got rid of the ones who weren't. They used to hold ceremonies in the basement, all of them naked, with cats and dogs for sacrifice . . . and maybe more. Once I was upstairs in my room, locked in, listening, and I'm sure I heard a baby crying downstairs. Then Dad came home suddenly, and there was a lot of screaming and bad words and things crashing. Then silence. I wanted to run away then, but my room was on the third floor and there was no place to go. I really did crawl out on the roof for a while . . . then Mom came to get me, still naked and covered with blood, and she said I knew too much and might as well know everything now. She and her friends took me down into the basement, and there was my dad, lying on the floor with black candles all around him. They'd cut out his heart."

Howard didn't say much for a while after that. He looked sick. Now he was the one who was scared. I was enjoying myself, shocked and ashamed that I was, like when you jerk off for the first time, but I enjoyed it anyway.

"They smeared his blood on my forehead, making signs, and then we all prayed, and we had to cut up his body and bury it under the basement floor, and some of it in the back yard, and it all had to be done before sunrise. And, you know . . . I was late for school that day."

I flashed a quick smile at Howard. He turned away as if I'd hit him.

I reached into the knapsack and touched.

We really were in the middle of nowhere now, alone in the darkness, in the pouring sleet and rain, with just the occasional car going by in the opposite lane. Outside, when I pressed my face to the glass, I couldn't find any warmth, any people, just miles and miles of muddy fields. Howard kept looking at me from the side, then looking away, and I knew what he was thinking. He was sure he'd got himself a cute little psycho, another Jack the Ripper or Jeffrey Dahlmer in the making if not in actual fact already. Maybe what I was telling him was true, kind of, only it wasn't my mom and I'd done all those things myself.

After what must have been hours we came to a little town where there was a diner open. Howard pulled into the parking lot, then got out. He leaned back into the car.

"You got to do anything?"

"No."

"You hungry? You want anything?"

"Uh, no."

He was shaking, and not just from the cold. "Well, I gotta . . . I have a lot of things I have to do."

I rested my head on my knapsack and smiled at him. "I'll be here. I want to be your friend."

He turned from me and ran into the diner. I sat there in the car, rocking back and forth gently, remembering, or making up my story, dreaming dreams of blood. I reached into the knapsack once more, and touched.

When Howard came back, maybe an hour later, he was the one who was quiet. He put a paper bag on the seat beside me. A burger and fries, for me. I didn't touch them. But I did reach out and take Howard's hand in mine.

"You're cold!" he said.

"Where are we going?"

"Just going. Maybe we'll find a motel."

He'd done what he had to do and decided what he had to decide, and we weren't going to the police, and he wasn't going to drop me off at the nearest mental hospital. At least not right away. Fine. It would be long enough.

"I forgot to tell you the rest of my story," I said.

"Yeah. You did."

"It got a lot worse when Mr. Andrescu arrived. He came in the night, for one of the ceremonies, and as soon as I saw him I was afraid of him, because he was . . . massive and hard, like a white marble statue that's come alive, and his eyes, there was something about his eyes like no eyes I'd ever seen before. Mom was afraid of him too, and the other ladies, but they went down into the basement with him anyway. I think the Devil sent him. I really do. I think they prayed to the Devil and that's why Mr. Andrescu came, but maybe they didn't really believe he would. Mom was crying. She told me to go up to my room and lock *myself* in, and barricade the door. She said she loved me, and gave me a hug and kissed me, and I tasted her tears, and there were so many things I wanted to say to her, hurt and angry things, but then she broke away and ran down into the basement with Mr. Andrescu and the rest. All that night I heard the screaming, not Mr. Andrescu, but the ladies, and when it was getting almost light Mom came to my room again. She had on her bathrobe and nothing else, and her face was like it had been when Dad beat her up. There was blood all over, but she didn't seem to be hurt, other than on her face, I mean. She said I had to help her because she was tired out and her arthritis wouldn't let her do everything that needed to be done. So down we went, and I had to help her bury Mrs. Walker, the lady from down the street who worked at the grocery store. Mrs. Walker's throat was all ripped out, and her heart was gone too. And we had to bury Mr. Andrescu *in a box* below the cellar floor. That was a lot of digging. Mom and the other ladies helped, but I did most of it. I didn't go to school at all that day, and when the job was done we all just slept and when it got dark again Mr. Andrescu was there and so was Mrs. Walker, and both of them were saying how darkness was so much better than light, and how we would all be in darkness one day and rule the darkened world—crazy stuff like that."

Howard jerked the wheel and banged on it so hard the horn blew.

"I'll say it's crazy. I don't know what really happened, Larry, or what those people did to you—and I think it must have been really terrible—but I *do* know that you *are* talking crazy stuff, because dead people don't come back to life or sleep daytimes in coffins under your basement floor—you're talking *vampires*, kid, and they only exist in movies. I think maybe you've seen too many movies, and your head is all screwed up and you don't know what's real and what isn't anymore."

We drove on, through the darkness and the storm, quiet again. I listened to the night and heard its voice, but the night was empty. There was only Howard. I slid over beside him and put my arm around him. He slid his arm around me, under my jacket, under my t-shirt.

"You're so cold you'll get sick," he said.

## DARRELL SCHWEITZER

I leaned my head on his shoulder. "Can we still be friends?"

He swallowed hard and nodded. "Yeah. We can be friends."

"You won't hurt me?"

He drew away quickly and gripped the wheel hard with both hands. "Oh, Larry . . . the ones I'm with, I *never* hurt them, *never*. I give them money and new clothes, whatever they want, but I *never* hurt them . . ."

"Then we can be friends?"

"Like I said, yes."

"Because Mr. Andrescu hurt me quite a lot. First he hurt Mrs. Dade and Mrs. Lovell and Mrs. Freeman, like he had Mrs. Walker, and we buried them all, and they all came back, every night, and sometimes there were others who came for the ceremonies, who died; but in the end it was only me and my mom living in the house by day, and I wanted to run away so bad, but Mom said no, because Mr. Andrescu could follow me anywhere and I mustn't make him mad. So Mr. Andrescu came for me in the end, one night, and he tore my bedroom door right off the hinges. I thought his eyes were on fire. They were like a wolf's eyes, all glowing with light. He carried me downstairs like I was a baby, crushing me. His arms felt like cold stone, but *alive*. 'Your mother saved you until the very last,' he said to me, 'but now you are mine.' I screamed for her, but she didn't answer, she didn't come and help me, and then she was there in the basement with all the other ladies. She hugged me one last time, and cried, and said how sorry she was that it had turned out this way, that she didn't want it to, but there was nothing she could do. I didn't believe her. I knew she could have done something. But she didn't. I cried too, and held her, and she was warm . . . then Mr. Andrescu pulled me away and he hurt me so much . . . They tore my clothes off and hung me up by the wrists from the pipes in

63

the ceiling . . . and first Mr. Andrescu cut open my legs and caught the blood in his hands. He drank some and gave it to the others, and they all drank, even my mother, though she wasn't dead yet, not like the others. If she had been, she wouldn't have been able to help herself, but she *wasn't*. They hurt me more, beat me with pieces of electrical cord . . . and they cut designs, *sigils*, into me with knives, and all of them were covered with my blood, rubbing it all over themselves and moaning. I screamed for my mom to help me, but she didn't, she didn't because she'd already sold her soul to Mr. Andrescu. Only when he was going to cut my heart out with his knife did she do anything. She tried to pull him away. She said he'd promised not to do that, and he only laughed and said it didn't make any difference anyway. I suppose it didn't, in the end."

Howard was the one who was crying, in the end. "You really are crazy, kid. You really are. You need help. Well we'll be friends and I'll see that you get help. I will. I promise."

"Look. There's a motel. Let's stop."

He glanced at his watch. "Nearly four in the morning. I guess we should."

"Yeah," I said.

And in the motel room, I showed him the marks Mr. Andrescu had made on my body, the *sigils*, and the ragged holes in my hands and feet. He and the ladies had nailed some boards together and actually crucified me in the basement. When I was hanging there, almost dead by feeling so much pain, Mr. Andrescu appeared out of a red mist, his eyes burning. He seemed to float in the air. He could make me like himself, he said, and I could live forever, and I wouldn't hurt anymore. Yes, I said, yes, please, make it stop, please, make it stop. And I called out to my mother then, but she didn't hear me, and Mr. Andrescu's arms crushed me like stone. I remember his eyes, gleaming in the red mist like two moons behind a thin layer of cloud.

When I told Howard all of my story, and even opened my knapsack and showed him what was inside, he was the one who did the screaming, but only briefly, before he died. When somebody knocked on the door and asked if we were all right, I said we were, it was only a bad dream. But it was the kind of bad dream that never ends, not for me, not for Howard, a dream he would go on dreaming too and try to understand, as I have tried to understand.

"It's not your fault," I told him. "It really isn't."

Maybe Mr. Andrescu could explain it all to him, tell him how we change, how I was still changing, how I hadn't run away from home at all, but had gone out into the world because Mr. Andrescu sent me, to propagate our kind. Those were his very words. And I had. I had made Howard like myself.

He was my first. I was still changing, from the boy my mother had sold in a useless attempt to save herself and Mr. Andrescu had murdered, into someone else, who went on, remembering and dreaming and continuing the story; the boy who wanted to go on loving his mother despite what she had done and somehow couldn't.

I tried, though. That was why I kept her head and carried it with me in my knapsack. In the daytime, when I slept in the sheltering darkness, I spoke to her in my dreams, and told her my story over and over, and she told me hers.

# Rock and Roll Will Never Die

E. J. GOLD

*Maybe those reports
of Elvis' death
were "exaggerated,"
after all.*

 DIDN'T WANT TO KILL Jim Morrison, but he insisted. Now, of course, he's a vampire, too. He still looks as good as the day he died; the bald spot hardly shows, and his food disorder is finally under control.

Hendrix and Joplin took it very gracefully—they knew I didn't want my victims to die, but how could I help it? If I bit them only once, they'd live forever; but my need for blood is, as you well know if you've studied the ancient lore, insatiable—at least by human standards.

Joplin's been in Ogden, Utah, since the day I killed her. She loves it there, where the bats fly free, and has been using the name "Harriet Sopworthy," up until last Wednesday, when, due to some misunderstanding about cattle mutilation (if we could live on cows' blood, would we have had so many problems with the living all these centuries?) she developed a sudden need to travel.

Hendrix is still an assistant copy editor at Time-Warner. He races boats, and recently released a new double album "Shock Absorber" on Yarrow Root, a small Indie label out of Duluth, Minnesota. Brain Epstein did the liner notes.

Morrison was one of the lucky ones. He'd signed an Automatic Resurrection Pact years before, so he was back on his feet in minutes, and as a rock star, the thing with the sunlight didn't affect him much; he was used to working nights.

Paul couldn't have been dead more than a couple minutes. He stayed on his feet the whole time, and wrote two songs the same afternoon, and nobody but a few gossip columnists ever knew the difference. And it's wrong to say that Paul is dead. He's very much undead.

Brian's every bit as undead as Paul; he's now the proud proprietor of a small but very exclusive antique shop on London's West End.

I was originally born into a nominally Jewish family, in French Hospital, New York, seven days after Pearl Harbor, for which I was not responsible.

Even though we weren't practicing Jews, it was definitely Judaism that saved me from a horrible fate worse than death; the first time a victim came after me with a crucifix, nothing happened.

I doubt that she understood me when I said, "Sie gar nicht helfen," and took her life's blood.

Passover? From Passover I knew nothing until spring of 1957, when I was sixteen, and had been invited to share a Seder—that's a ritual Jewish dinner you have at home with relatives and prayer.

I'd always thought of Passover as a sort of Jewish Easter. I spent this one with my cousins Sandi, Ricky, Henny and Keith, and my wonderful and loving Aunt Greta and Uncle Floyd.

I can't even say "Floyd." It was my uncle Floyd who, on his seven-hundred and thirty-fifth birthday, just as he and his new bride Marcie (also a vampire) were about to fly off to Europe for the weekend, suddenly wants to be called by his middle name "Cliff." Who can remember "Cliff"?

Don't get me wrong. Not all my relatives are vampires. My cousin Audrey (who moved to Ireland and currently lives alone in a small, cramped damp and moldy cottage in County Wicklow, Ireland) is the only one of us who actually left in her Will that she explicity refused to be buried facing Macy's.

My entire family, of course, expected me to become a doctor. What else? I was obviously too intelligent to be a lawyer, and nobody but a *nudnik* would want a dentist in the family these days.

The thing is, just plain "doctor" wasn't enough for them; a regular doctor is always on call, has to work nights—and what marriage can stand that? Believe me, grandchildren are always at the root of any Jewish family planning.

My parents wanted me to be a *specialist*, focusing on diseases of the very rich. But who had the time (I had to work for a living during my middle teens) or the money (for a decent medical school with postgraduate work it cost a hundred-thousand even *then*).

*Now*, when I don't need it, with the knowledge of anatomy I've garnered from countless victims, and the geriatrics (you wouldn't believe the problems, of which anemia is the least) I picked up everywhere from Dr. MacDougall to Susan Powter, even without medical school, I could be a doctor.

I *could* be a doctor, if I wasn't so squeamish about blood, but I am. I suppose it's some form of guilt.

I can't imagine where such guilt could possibly come from. But by the time I waded through three failed marriages (I eat lots of late-night snacks) and dozens of weekend Life-Repair Seminars at Esalen in Big Sur (I had to drop a rock on Dick Price's head from above—a super-feat for a tiny bat—to make it look like an accident, as if he'd been hit by a falling stone while meditating under a cliff) in the mid-70's, the guilt got so bad I couldn't stare another jugular vein in the face.

But who cares *why* the guilt. I'm a vampire, and that's that. I guess it was some sort of genetic Jewishness, even though we weren't practicing Jews, that began to assert itself at about the twentieth victim. I think Hefner went through pretty much the same thing.

It wasn't guilt that drove Jim Morrison into Judaism. It was fear of the Cross. After those horrible attacks by a mob of rabid crucifix-bearing born-again christians in Tyler, Texas back around 1974, he converted.

But that didn't last long. I met him at the Brooklyn Botanical Gardens on a cross-country feeding expedition one summer night in 1983; he'd left the Yeshiva, following a bloody run-in with an inter-ethnic mob on the corner of King's Highway and Avenue L.

Apparently, he'd sounded the wrong click. When the debs flashed their long, wavy stainless-steel blades, he'd flashed his fangs.

He always fancied himself to be heavily oriented toward the darkside, but the fact is, Jaimie was more an anti-establishment rebel than a Satanist, though he'd hate it to become generally known, and Christianity was the only establishment he'd been taught to see.

Believe me, even Alice Cooper (who never felt a thing and was already thoroughly undead by the time he walked into the Psychedelic Supermarket on Las Palmas where I stalked victims during the Summer of Love) couldn't have spooked these Bushwick Babes, and the whole gang came after him waving everything they had on chains around their necks.

Morrison finally got smart. Now, you couldn't get him with a cross, Star of David, *mezuza, chai, figa, corno* or mojo bag.

Hazel wand? Blasting Rod? Athame? There's no piece of religious hardware known that can stop him now. Not even a silver bullet. He's switched to Zen.

What are you asking? Of *course* I can fly like a bat...and don't try to trick me into shapeshifting into something small, so you can smash me with some nearby heavy object like that telephone over there on the night table.

I'm unkillable. I've had plenty of time to learn how to be. Besides, I don't mean you any harm. Actually, you're going to be immortal. And when you're immortal, after I've drunk your blood, you'll learn how to be unkillable, too, and you may even learn to like it.

You want to know about flying skills? I'll tell you about flying skills. They came in very handy, I can tell you, when I put Lynyrd Skynnyrd, Rick Nelson and Jim Croce on "empty" in midair. It wasn't easy to get out of Nelson's private aircraft, and I crashed with it.

Naturally, everybody survived, if you call this living.

Elvis was an easy kill, a pathetic creature, lying there on the bathroom floor with a bible clutched in one hand and a bottle of Demarol in the other. I told him to get plastic surgery, but as you well know, he's been spotted just about everywhere.

He can't seem to stay away from populated areas where he'd be easily recognized. The King always did have a big appetite, even after he hit the drugs, and to a vampire, blood isn't just chopped liver.

Buddy Holly and the Big Bopper? They were before my time. They were taken out by Myrna Loy. I only happen to know because it was she who robbed me of my daylight life, in the anteroom of the Temple Beth-El on 14th and Second Avenue. We met there every Saturday morning snuggling happily together as she sucked on my vein and drained me to chalky whiteness in the darkness of the cloakroom.

As far as my mother and father knew, on Saturdays I was safely tucked away on some side balcony (I always thought superman was skinny until I reached puberty and was allowed to sit in the Loge) at one of the 14th Street movie theaters (which still had live, onstage vaudeville between the cliff-hangers and the short subjects).

She was very gentle with me, and it was to her patience and bird-like appetite that I attribute the fact that I am that rare victim who survives a vampire's repeated attacks long enough to become one of the *Kinder von den Nacht.*

Everyone thinks Philly Joe Jones was the one who took down Buddy Holly, but Philly Joe had a gig at the Blue Note that night, (our band opened for the Jazz Messengers and MJQ that year) so he had a tableside alibi; me.

There were others, many others, who were my victims. One loses track in the roiling wake of victims. And to be honest, these days, to me, all humans look alike.

I didn't mean to kill "Mama" Cass Elliot, either, and it wasn't my fault. She was right next door, eating a very attractive kosher tuna sandwich on Levi's rye bread. I was tempted, but I can't touch tuna fish, and it's not just the mercury.

Between my excema and my diverticulosis, all I need is more rancid oil in my system. I still eat food and I drink nonalcoholic beverages. Naturally, I never drink . . .wine . . .

Why do I eat and drink, even though I don't have to? I'm a member of the Academy of Motion Picture Arts and Sciences. Can you imagine me going to an Academy luncheon, sitting across the table from Oliver Stone and Joyce and Kurt Kenyon and not eating *anything*?

It's bad enough, my publicist has to deal with the Bulemia rumors in the tabloid press. Things like that cost a bundle to fix, and unless you get the negatives, they don't *stay* fixed.

It had gotten very hot for me in L.A. and the East Coast was still buzzing with excitement over my last feasting, when my record company, who'd loused up both the cover of our new album (which is why it went out with no graphics whatever) *and* our Frankfurt booking, flew me to London for the first leg of our tour (the *Laughing Wolves* had come onto the charts that week with "Round Midnight" at twenty-seven with a bullet) and I'd found a little flat at number 11 Curzon Place, which was just close enough to Harrad's department store to suit my light, on-the-road shopping needs.

Imagine my surprise to find that Keith Moon was my next-door neighbor! Keith went quickly—generally they don't pass into final slumber until the sixth or seventh bite. This had absolutely no bad effect, however, and with any luck, *halilah*, he'll continue to be the best guitarist in the business.

I still run into him now and then at one of our favorite feeding grounds (the Vatican is now considered a Protected Vampire Sanctuary).

I'd lived next door to Number 9 for a couple months, (it's now owned by Pete Townshend to protect it from human contamination) when Cass decided on a whim to stay there during a London concert appearance, rather than have to endure the misery of a commercial London hotel, even a good one.

Here she had some privacy from the papparazzi and TV journalists, the hangers-on, groupies, newswire stringers and "wannabe" songwriters. It was also here that she had a private kitchen, and that was why the tuna sandwich.

If it hadn't been for the aroma of that tuna sandwich wafting across the way, I'd never have been able to go on, because it was Mama Cass who gave me the idea that saved the lives of all my victims since that day.

I loved Cass, and wouldn't have hurt her for the world. We'd been introduced by Sky Saxon, and my friend Jon, who danced with Vito, a venerable sculptor/bodhisattva who invented body-painting and freakouts, and Cass and I had become good friends.

We used to get high together, and with Michelle, John, Vito, Leda, Frank, Al, Alice and Famous Gene (who was the acid connection) and drive up to Lake Malibu to watch the flying saucers land.

I had intended to confer immortal life on Mama Cass (whose name came more from her membership in "the Mamas & the Papas" than her "Venus of Villendorf" figure, at the suggestion of Fred and Martha Adler, two adorable Gardnerian wiccans.

At her ponderous Rubensian womanliness, she needed *something*, and I thought immortality would fit the bill. How could I have known she had Angina and would have a heart attack when she saw my fangs?

"Look at this newspaper clipping from the Corpus Christi *Times!*" she'd murmured as I'd bent fondly over her invitingly pulsating neck. Then, suddenly, she slumped over on the big brass bed on which Keith Moon had expired under my hypnotic spell only a short while earlier.

I knew a cardiac infarction when I saw one. Believe me, this was not a person choking on a sandwich.

"Hold on," I encouraged, using my Dracula Family Crest Decoder Ring (we can't communicate in the open, of course, and digital encryption devices cost an arm and a leg) to administer slight shocks to her throat, as I'd thought vaguely I'd seen some doctor do somewhere in the distant past.

Finally it came to me. It wasn't in Columbia University Medical School as I'd first supposed (they used to lock people out of John Jay Hall if you were a few seconds after curfew).

I saw the scene clearly now; Bela Lugosi leaning concernedly over Glenn Strange, who was lying helplessly against the ice, in *Abbott & Costello Meet Frankenstein*.

I watched Cass as she lay on the big brass bed, her beautiful *saftig* face relaxed in the gentle release of death.

I realized I had only nanoseconds to react. Biting deeply into her throbbing carotid artery, I held her wrist gently; soon that terrifyingly mortal pulse was gone, replaced by the nice, steady coolness of the undead.

I managed to get the vampire enzyme—or whatever it is that turns you into a vampire or a werewolf once you've been bitten—into her jugular vein, long before she was brain-dead, or she wouldn't be walking the streets (and flying the airwaves) now.

Like Morrison, she never looked better than she does today and, like most of my vampire friends, she's into Zen and jogging.

Last week, she visited me at my mountain retreat where we cut some background vocals for my new album "Only Sleeping," the profits from which were largely eroded by excessive studio time, according to the record company execs and, as usual, they can't locate the spread sheets.

As I stood over her, waiting for her to revive (she was back up on her feet soon enough to accompany me on a shopping spree that very afternoon—like natural childbirth—I finally had a panic-free moment in which to read the press clipping from the Corpus Christi *Times*:

TIME SHARE NEW CRAZE AMONG YUPPIES, read the headline. It wasn't front page, but to me, it meant escape from the shame and disgust I felt every time I drained the last drop of blood from some victim I'd kept lingering pale and wan, weak and weary, over tedious months and years.

Imagine that! From just a little headline on a two-column-inch story from the family section of a Corpus Christi, Texas newspaper, I obtained, not the secret of life—what good would that have done me?—but the secret of half-life.

Cass was right; I wouldn't ever have to kill—and feel that horrible *guilt* about killing—ever again. I could be a vampire and still have my self-esteem.

Could that have been what Dick Price was trying to murmur at that last, lingering moment when I drained the final drop of blood from his slowly crumpling form?

Believe me, he's a lot better off busing tables at Lieberman's Resort in Mount Freedom, New Jersey, than running a broken-down 70's encounter center converted from your typical Big Sur motel (I think either he or Michael Murphy inherited, but what do I know from these New Age *megillahs*?).

And could it have been what David Crosby was trying to tell me, his eyes bugging with horror, when he pulled that handgun on me backstage as I went for his half-screaming throat? He's a family man, now; they tell me his memory of that event isn't good; so I guess I'll never know.

Could those have been the final words gasped by Forry Ackerman when he crumpled beneath my bloodlusting spell? Or was it, as some say, "What some authors won't do to save a lousy ten percent!"?

Why am I telling you this, you ask? I'll tell you why. My current husband is a nice guy; a good provider, not very rough in bed, sensitive, kind, good sense of humor, doesn't have more than three affairs a year.

I wouldn't want to lose him over a thing like this. But he's very straight. A country-clubber. What does he know from PMS, quiet non-urgent hugging, and unwanted facial hair? Believe me, he wouldn't understand you and me, two women, in bed together.

Don't be afraid. I'm actually doing you a *mitzvah*—a favor.

E. J. GOLD

I'm going to bite you on the neck.

*Now.*

There . . . That didn't hurt, did it? It's the hypnosis; gives you a feeling of euphoria. Lots of victims—especially R&B musicians—ask for a second and a third, just for the rush.

On my word you can rely; a vampire's bite comes on stronger, and hits heavier peaks, than pure Sandoz liquid acid. But a kid like you—what are you, honey, maybe thirtyish? You're welcome—what do you kids today know from psychedelics?

Twenty minutes from now, you'll be a vampire, just like me and all my rock musician, film industry and science fiction publishing friends. But don't worry. Not only will you be immortal, you'll have the secret of obtaining reasonably fresh human blood without having to ever kill a victim.

What? Another hit? Sure . Here's your timeshare punch-card. We rotate between victims, allowing them to bounce back. And unlike our ancestors, we pay them for the privilege. All our donors are screened and tested regularly, not that human diseases will ever affect you again, but it's a strictly kosher club.

Which means you can't fly on Saturdays. And you can't drink blood and milk together.

As a new member, you get an automatic 1000 hours, and a hundred shares of stock. As a matter of fact, are you in luck! Our TimeShare BloodClub just went public at 64-1/8. You should *see* this prospectus!

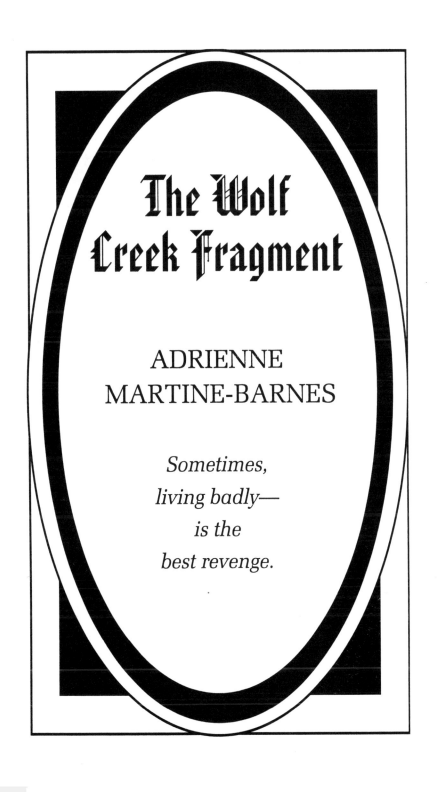

# The Wolf Creek Fragment

## ADRIENNE MARTINE-BARNES

*Sometimes,
living badly—
is the
best revenge.*

EMO: TO JOEL BRITTEN:

Here is all I could recover of that journal I told you about on the phone. The pages seem authentic—we tested them at Carnegie and the paper is certainly nineteenth century, as well as the binding. It is a typical ante-bellum commonplace book, and the handwriting is consistent with that of someone who had attended a little of some dame's school between say 1840-1860. Beyond these verifiable facts I refuse to hazard any guesses.

As I told you, I found this journal in the still warm remains of what looked like a small settlement while I was hiking in the Shenandoah Mountains. The town, if it was a town, had been burnt within a day or so of my arrival—damn good thing the entire forest didn't catch! I found some axeheads and pots that survived. I also found the burnt skeletons of several adults. I didn't stay to play detective. I just went over to Jay's Crossing and called the state police.

I knew of your interest in cases like the one described here—at least I assume this is authentic. Or, rather, I can't imagine anyone going to the extent of attempting a hoax of this magnitude in the middle of nowhere, and hoping a patsy would be hiking by at the right time to find this book. l don't have a clue if the place was burnt out by the inhabitants, by the folks from nearby, or by parties unknown. (The townsfolk from Jay's Crossing were unfriendly, bordering on hostile—so l didn't ask too many questions.)

Let's discuss it when I get to Philly next, over some of your good sherry.

Sincerely,<br>
Bruce Pickering

No day goes by I don think bout what we did, an what a bitty thing she was. It been eating at me for so long, so Jacob set me to puttin down what I member.

Strong and bitty—how she tore at us an lickt the scratches and bit us. We wus all to drunk to feal it, me an Carl and Zeb an Jacob, to drunk an to stupid to think. Her licks burnt my skin lik fyre, so I hit her. I never hit a woman befor nor sinct. Zeb, he banged her pur hed on a rok, an she hisst lik a rattler, an her greeny eyes got funny. I wisht I kud furgit, an I wisht we hadna dun it. Jus caus we wus so drunk an she were alone an a stranger werent no scuse. I kan heer her a screamin, til ol Zeb he kut her hed off with his Daddys ax. He alwus wus a meen one, Zebulon wus. We all figgered no one wud never no bout no bitty, dark gal wlth no kin that we layed with an kilt. We dug down a littel an shoved dirt over her body—she wur so small—an Zeb put her hed in a feed sack and tosst it inna Wulf Creek. The moon was hi, an her blood cum otta that sack an made the water dark. An we swore we wudden say about it, an we dint, even after the hunger came. Not for a long time.

## ADRIENNE MARTINE-BARNES

Ma an Pa rayst me an Carl as good as they kud, bi the Book. I no my Skriptur, and I no not to steel or kill or covet. I did that one bad thing, an I knowd Id burn for it. But I never nowd bout anythin like the hunger. It aint in the Book. I dint never think there wur things that wusent in the Book. The Life Everlastin is promist after we die—which never made no cents to me, but Preecher tol us—but this here livin an livin and never gettin no older—I jus don rightly no how that kud happen. Thst bitty gal lookt 12 or 13, so I don no how old she relly wus. I hate to think she was a hunnert.

Jacob reeds better an me—he got more skoolin an he was right smart to begin. He figgert out we got a sickness from that bitty gal. Alwus has his hed in some book, does Jacob. Hes got sum way to rite away to somewheres, an after a wile, theres a big box on the stump by the Crossin an we put it on our wagon an bring it back. I askt him what he yewes fur money, an he jus smiles. Zeb, he kudden reed worth a dam, and he wus alwus a bad un, even when we wus jus boys runnin round in the woods, been foolish. Zeb was born meen an bad, an we follert him caus he were meen an bad. He wus big an onery an ful o the Devil, I spose. But he was kin—Ma wus his aunty— so he wus here a lot, inna mischiff like a coon.

Me an Carl wus reel ordnary, mos the time. We did chores an et suppers—I aint et no supper in morna hunnert years now, caus the hunger makes you siken from vittels, like. An I aint had a drop a likker sinct that night. Ive wanted it, but I no it don keep down. I dint think bout nun a this til Jacob set me to puttin it down—me with jus the to yeers a daym skool, back before the War. I never rit this many words in my life afore. Sometimes I kan almos taste Mas chicken an biskits, or greens an bacon, an I wisht I had em to eat now. Corse Mas been in the churchyard sinct 1859, rest her good soul. She never new what we dun, so she was spared e lot of greef, an spared the hunger an the torment by that kwinzy. She got the Life Everlastin, an we jus got the torment. I want to die—Jacob an me both. I dunno what Carl wants. He don talk no more. We jus stay here at the Creek, with the hunger eatin at us, an the hole town a hatin at us—I spose the Lord is just.

Zeb, now. He went away. When the War started, he scatted. By then, he wurent Zeb no more. I don rightly no what he wus—Jacob might—but he werent no one we wanted fur kin. I spose he werent right in his hed to start, an the hunger worsent it. He wus so big and slow, an after he kut the hed offen that bitty gal, he werent the least sorry. He never seemt to feal no shame in it. But after, he seemt to get a kunnin in him, likt the hunger smartent him sum.

We all kep reel kwyet an did our chores an went to church an pretendet like we wus good boys. We wus all awaitin for sum kin o that bitty gal to kum round, asskin for her. When no one did, we got a mite ezzyur, and then, bout a week or like after, we all got reel sick an we kudden keep down no food at all. Carl an me jus lay in our bed there, up under the eves, and burnt. I never nood a body kud get so hot. I think Hell mus be like that. Meenwhiles, one a Dan Breakstones hounds dun fownt the body o tha bitty gal, an even sick as we wus, Carl and me herd the ol'hens waggin theer tungs an a kluking away over it. Wulf Creek aint never been very big, an the lees littel thing kan caus a lotta tawk. I member when Mrs MacFearson had twins, everyon tawkt, an when one died, they tawkt mor. Zeb thot he wus so kleever, puttin the hed in the creek, but the resta her had sumthin to tell.

Any ol' woodsman like Dan kan tell purty good how long a things been ded. It don need no booklearnin, like I heer they got nowadays. Leestwize Jacob says there be thing they kan do with ol dirt or flesh or bones, and that there be folks who spent ther hole lives puttin bits in bottles an a testin at em. Seams to me a funny way to put vittels on the table, but hits honest work, I spose. Dan never put no dirt in a jar—he just looked at that gal and nowd shed aben in the grownd a purty good wile.

Cept she wur still fresh. There werent no korrupshun, cept the brewez on her littel legs, an' where we hit her. He wus right befuddelt. She werent buryt reel deep, but no bugs had et at her, an no birds or critters neether. His ol hownd took 1 wiff an bakt off—l member him tellin Pa that, up on the front steps. An Pa gimme such a stare, like he nowd maybee I dun sumthin bad. I wus jus up from siknin an I wisht I was back abed an throwin up my vittels sted a sittin thcrc with my Pa lookin at me like I wus a bug. Carl he lookt bout reddy to cry, but he kep his tung behin his teeth. We swore we wudna say nuthin to no one. But it was reel hard caus we was full a hunger an week an our heds was stufft with the memberin. That bitty gal was almos poyntin her finger at us from that grave we dug.

They put together a decent coffyn, an sum a the wimmen done her a fair windin cloth, an put her in a corner of the churchyard. Sumtimes, when I go to talk to Ma an Pa under thier stone, I go over an tell that bitty gal how sorry I am. I take her flowers when I ken get em. There wus a few ol' biddies dint want her buried, a caus she were defylt, but Preecher said we wus Christians, and hadent no business tryin to The Lords work for him. I dunno why, but I tuk comfort from that. I dint no I wudent get to chance to see Heven nor Hel.

Soon afters I wus walkin in the south field, an I was so hungry in my belly I kudda cryd, cept it wudda shamed me. I member lookin at one of the caffs, an my hed gettin all whirlee like I just went an put my teeth on that caffs neck and bit down hard as I kud. My teeth went in so ezzy I wus surprist—right down thru the skin. I kud smell the hide nex to my ol nose. That caff bellert reel hard. I spose it hurt. But the blood kum inna my mouth, an I drunk it down til my belly stopt hurtin. I lickt that blood offen my mouth an lookt to see that no one had seen me. That caff lookt at me so sad, lik that bitty gal, an I kudden look at it. But it dint seem nun the worse, an I felt strong agin.

It wusent til supper that I reely thot bout bitin that caff—when I kudden get down no chops an waxbeens. I membert how that gal had bit us, lik I bit the caff. It sure made Zeb mad, all her bitin wile we helt her down. It lef sores lik skeeter bites. I kep tryin to eat, an so did Cark but I felt so sick I hadda stop. An Pa lookt at me agin, an I think he new then that I had sumthin to do with that gal we put inna churchyard. He dint say nuthin. Pa never wus one fur talkin.

I told Carl bout suckin the caffs blood, an how it fillt me up good, and his eyes went all roundy. He lookt reel pail in the lite from our candel. An we both just layed their on our bed that nite, an a lot o nites afters. He musta tol Jacob, caus he askt me a lot of kweshuns after church the nex Sunday. Every fuw days Id sneek over an suck on that caff, an feel better. But that hunger kep ot me, so I lookt at my sisters necks funny, an even at Pa an Ma.

That caff, it sickened a littel, an fell over ded one mornin. It wur a sore loss. We wusent dirt poor like sum folks, caus Ma cum well dowert from her folks down in Richmund, but we wusent so rich we kud los our caff ezy. I member Pa a standin by that pur beast, his brow all puckert, an a shakin his hed. We burnt it, an the smell made me reel sic. I felt reel bad bout that caff, an bout the bitty gal agin.

### ADRIENNE MARTINE-BARNES

Zeb, he got reel wild bout then. His Ma was long gone, an his Pa had got a new bryde, womman nama Polly White from over by Kovinton. She was rite fine—purty an sweet an not much oldern Zeb. I member she had this dimity dres she wor on warm days—she give my sister Betty suma the skraps fur a kwilt—an alwus lookt tidy an kul. Ma sayd she was a reel lady, an Ma new bout that, cummin from Richmund like she done. Polly wus alwus smilin or laffin, and she made Unkel Jethro smile to.

Well, Zeb he got sum kinna fit, an one day he jus tore that dimity dress offen his new Ma an thru her onna floor and did like we did to the bitty gal. He lef her half ded an all biten an nekkid. Jethro fownd her, an he went after Zeb an shot him inna belly. Zeb got up like nuthin happen an beat his own Pa to deth with the stock a that gun. He tol us after church on Sunday. In a day his belly wur fine, an no one fownd out rite aways. Zeb gave out that Jethro had gon down to Richmund a sudden like, an Polly was abed with sum womman thing. He had got reel kunnin from the hunger. No one got to nosy, and he tuk his Pa's wagon over to the Crossin an burnt it an lef Jethro's body in the woods, like a robber had kilt him. I dint wanna no, but Zeb made us lissen. He seemt to be reel prowd of hisself, an Carl an me jus went away. At first we thot he wur yarnin sum bout that belly shot, but then I kut my hand onna scyth, an the kut stopt bleedin reel fast, an the kut was gone inna mornin. We talkt to Jacob, an he sayd the sickness dun made us strong sumhow.

Polly, she got well after a bit, but she dint smile no more, an folks started a tawkin that maybe her an Zeb dun away with Jethro. The wimmen gossipt, but no one dun anythin. Zeb. he went sparkin after every gal in town, an the tawk died down sum. Polly, she jus sat inna rocker an lookt inna corner, an sum ol biddy sayd she musta lost a child an was greevin sumthin fyerce. But pur Polly had the hunger an she had it reel bad. Jacob figgert it out an tol us. We wus fulla sikeness, an we new it now.

Ma sikent that winter, as wus tuk off by the kwinzy, so she never hadda find out what her sons hadda dun to that there bitty gal. She never saw that ol' hunger goin round the town, goin to an fro, like the Devil. I be glad she wus spared, an onlee wisht I cudda ben spared to.

Cum spring, haf the gals an summa the fellers hadda got that ther hunger. Sum died with the sikeness of it, and sum cum thru just fine. I don no why, an Jacob dont neether. Then Zeb he tol what we dun to sum gal, how we hadda kilt that bitty gal. Preecher called a meetin at the church, to decyde what to do with us. Everyone came cept me an Zeb an Carl an Jacob. Pa tol us to stay away, an Preecher tol Zeb the same Those what had the hunger sat on one side, and them wlthout sat on the other, an Preecher callt fur order. Preecher wus rite powerful—he wus the bigest man I ever saw, cept Zeb—an he hadda voyce lik thundr. He tol everyone we kudent let this here hunger get loows, an we better not be tellin anyone frum the Crossin or Frowst what we got, or theyd cum an kil us. I wisht they hadda.

They jabbert all nite. Carl an me kud see the lanturns burnin in the church. When they wus dun, they decydet that them who din't have the hunger should leeve and move away, an them what had it would stay in Wulf Creek. They come an tol us that they wus good Christians, so they wusn't gonna hang us, but we kudent cum to church no mor, an we kudent marry no gals, a caus we wus defylt. Then they tol us no one in town wus ever gonna spek to us agin—that wus hard. Preecher convinced em to let the Good Lord do the judgen when we

ADRIENNE MARTINE-BARNES

died. So, most of those what werent sick went over to Leroy or the Crossin, but a few like Pa stayed in Wulf Creek.

I'd ruther theyd a hung us, to say the trewth, caus the hunger kep us livin an livin. But no one new or gessed, not even Jacob who is reel smart, that we got no way to die less we do it ourseffs. Ma and Pa wus lucky—they died naturel. Them as got the hunger an died frum it rite off was lucky to. But the resta us go on an on, for forevers as neer as we kan tell. Only good thing is we done get us no babies, even them that wus married. That wus a sore greef to the wimmen, not to hav the comfort of a child. We don get hurt an we don get no older, lik we is froze by the hunger. We keep up a good herd a cattle and sum goats fur food, an never see no one from one yeer to the nex. Sum boys in brown kum thru bout 15 summers back, an we all watcht them til they went off into the woods. They wus singin and wearin bags on theer shoulders. Jacob says they wus Boy Scowts and that they go offen the woods fur fun. I think the wirld mus be very strange now.

Sum a us has gone plum crazy. Caleb Smith he kilt his wife an son, bout forty years back, then hung hisself. My brother Carl been a sittin in our Pas room, a starin at the walls, for ner on sixty yeers. He don tawk no more—just drink his blood when I carry it up tos him. The rest—them as aint crazy or hasent kilt theirselfs—go on, mindin the stock an hatin us. I don spose it will ever end.

Sumtimes, at nite, I sit on the porch an look at the moon and wonder what things wudda been lik if I hadent got drunk with Zeb. An I wonder what happent to him, when he went offen to the War. I sur hope he got his hed blowt offen with a cannonball or wus hung. But mosly . . .

# Visiting the Neighbors

## JANRAE FRANK

*It sounds innocent enough. . .*

CE CRUSTED TREES—mostly pines and mountain ash—splashes of green filled the view from the black cadillac's windows. I refused to sit up for a clearer view, though usually I liked to watch the trees flash by. But I felt as furious as the snow that flurried in angry swirls among the trees. I curled into a sulky ball against the soft black velvet seat my knees drawn up against the car door, my waist still cinched by the seatbelt though I had evaded the clutch of the shoulder harness. I pictured myself as a cat— a large, sinuous orange tabby just the color of my hair, an indignant tabby. Mama was abandoning me again to go hunting in Europe—though she wouldn't call it that when she talked to the neighbors. No, she would have a perfectly good excuse for dumping me on their doorstep: Such as my delicate health, my asthma, my allergies, she simply couldn't take me into all those awful pollens (I'd never been sick a day in my life); or she had enrolled me in Summer School-camp and I was *SO* counting on it. Ich!

The car picked up speed. The tires grinding and sliding despite the heavy chains: The chains weren't made for these speeds and the car wasn't built for this kind of weather. But Mama feared neither men, machinery or nature. The caddie, although beautiful, was terribly old-fashioned in these days of soaring gasoline prices—just like Mama. She bought it when she was living in Heidelberg and *visiting* the professors. The caddy would go back to Europe with her if it survived. Just then I wanted more than anything to scream how I hated the car, hated Mama, and especially hated going to visit the neighbors! I loathed these trips. Everytime she decided to go hunting in Europe she dumped me on a new set of people— usually ones I hadn't even met before! I was determined to force her into admitting I had a legitimate grievance.

"Oh, Mama!" I protested, staring now at the ceiling and door. "I really wish you would quit dumping me on strange people!" My next words were lost as the racing caddie lurched suddenly against a deep rut. The wheels ground for a moment, then Mama shifted the transmission into reverse and backed up.

"Melisande!"

I flinched. Her sharp, whip-like tone stung: Mama could be simply savage at times. I tilted my head and regarded her from the corner of my eyes. Mama's dark blue eyes flashed angrily in a pale face with her heavy black hair swept up into a delicate lacy pile of curls. I wondered briefly how I would look wearing my chestnut locks in that style—I would try it when she wasn't around.

"Melisande! And where would you have us live? The village is gone, the schloss is in disrepair!" Mama threw me a quick indignant glance "Would you have us live in tents?"

I winced at her tone, but refused to yield the point. "No, but we could fix the roof. Or stay at the ranch. I like the ranch."

"Melisande, the hunting is poor at the ranch We haven't caught anything worth eating in weeks."

"It's not Melisande, it's Melissa! I hate Melisande!"

"Melisande is a family name! My great-aunt Melisande, your namesake, was a countess in the Old Country."

"The Old Country! I'm absolutely sick of hearing about it. I've never been there. I don't want to go there. And you're not listening to me! You don't know how humiliating all this is— Besides you don't make Alexandra go visit the neighbors! Why should I be the only one who goes to visit the neighbors?"

Mama kept looking angrily back at me over her shoulder as she answered. "Now, Melisande, you know I can't do a thing with your sister since your father left. She runs off every time the subject comes up."

Mama yanked the wheel furiously around almost sideswiping a big pine tree. "Mama, watch the road, please! You're scaring me!"

"Oh, Shut up, Melisande! I know what I'm doing! You are going to stay with the neighbors. And that is the end of it!"

Just then I saw a disintegrating stone fence half buried in the snow. We had drifted off the road in the unplowed white brilliance and that stone fence just seemed to rise up as suddenly as the devil's own.

"Mama! Look out! You're going to hit it!"

Then she saw it too and swerved so sharply the caddie began to spin. Round and round the car went—it seemed forever— then we smashed into a tree.

I MUST HAVE STRUCK MY HEAD, because I woke up in bed with a plump, pleasant faced woman, her long brown hair twisted into a conservative bun, bending over me. She held my hand, patting it solicitously.

I didn't have to ask to know: Mama, car and all were gone.

A handsome middle-aged man with an old-fashioned square

clipped beard, stood beside the woman. "My dear child, we are relieved to see you are feeling better. We've all been concerned about you." he said in a refined Southern voice. "I'm Joseph Andrews. This," he added, indicating the plump woman, "Is my housekeeper, Mrs. Lafontaine. You'll stay with us until your mother can return for you. We're neighbors you know. Our ranch is are only about twenty miles south of yours."

I sat up in bed and Mrs. Lafontaine immediately shoved pillows behind my back. I settled against them, chewing my lower lip, thoughtfully. I remembered Mama talking about Mr. Andrews over the last year and a half since we'd come to live in Montana. He was a member of one of those fundamentalist Survivalists groups that were scattered through the state. "Um huh. Mama talked about you."

Mr. Andrews bent closer to me with a solicitous smile on his face and I could smell rancid maleness beneath the layers of deodorant and Old Spice. It took a real effort not to gag. "you'll be just fine here, Melisande, my dear."

"Melissa, please. Not Melisande, it's so pretentious. It's—" I groped for the right word, one that strike just the proper note with this strangely old-fashioned man. "It's just not American, if you know what I mean, Mr. Andrews?"

Mr. Andrews smiled. "So be it then, Melissa. My daughter Emily is just your age. It gets lonely at this ranch. I'm sure she will enjoy your company."

"Yes, Mr. Andrews." I managed to smile. "I'm sure I will too." I said. But silently I was cursing the fate called Mama that had me visiting the neighbors again.

Mr. Andrews, an expatriate Texan, owned the old Von Heidenstram ranch. Mama's car had overturned practically on his front lawn . Needless to say, I was not at all happy about the situation. Not only were they strangers to me, but they were Fundamentalists! It was worse than I had dreamed possible. The whole situation was an absolute nightmare! And knowing Mama, she had probably convinced him that we shared his beliefs completely. Gawd! Why did she keep doing this to me?

Mrs. Lafontaine clicked off the lamp on the old fashioned claw-footed nightstand as they withdrew. Just before they reached the door I glimpsed a slender blonde girl outlined in the doorway. Like Mrs. Fontaine she wore her hair pulled tightly back in an unfashionable bun that made her face look pinched and plain. I suspected that a little make-up and a more flattering hair style would make a big difference. I guessed that must be Emily. But Mrs. Lafontaine whisked her away before I could tell any more about her. Nevertheless I found something disturbingly attractive about the girl.

I worried all night about whether or not I could manage to fit in among the Andrews! I was also intensely distraught over the possibility that Emily might not like me. That I might not meet her expectations. I know that makes no logical sense—she was only a shadow glimpsed in a doorway—but I did.

I WOKE IN THE EARLY MORNING, hours before my accustomed time, in response to a tentative tap on my bedroom door. "Come in," I said.

Emily pushed the door slightly open and smiled uncertainly around the edge of the door, wavering a moment as with some desperate indecision.

"Come in," I called. "I'm not going to bite you, you know."

"I didn't think you would!" Emily blurted, then clapped her hands over her mouth, blushing deeply as she stepped into the room. "Mrs. Lafontaine sent me to tell you breakfast is ready."

I smiled, thinking Emily was so beautiful and young and fresh. Such a soft, sweet girl! Rather like spun sugar, hair like butter frosting and a hint of strawberries about her lips and lovely cheeks. I would always remember the taste of sugar, butter frosting and strawberries when I thought of Emily years afterward. That was definitely how Emily tasted to me.

"You're not afraid of me, surely not?"

Emily shook her head. A wisp of blonde hair escaped its bounds slid around the left side of her face. For just a moment her expression was so appealing that it quickened my pulse. For just a moment I forgave Mama for making me visit the neighbors: this particular visit might prove enjoyable after all.

Then Emily, with an almost frightened abruptness seized that loose strand of hair that so attracted me, snatched a bobby pin from her pocket and secured it to her bun. Something in that gesture made me feel uneasy and uncertain. There was something about Emily that I just couldn't interpret—I'm very good at reading people or I would never have survived so many visits—but for me she was both disturbingly unreadable and mesmerizingly attractive. The more I looked at her, the more I wanted Emily to like me.

We simply stared at each other for several minutes. The silence was swiftly reaching the point of rudeness on Emily's part—she being the hostess—when she finally spoke again.

"I am sorry, Melissa. I don't mean to stare," Emily apologized. "You remind me of someone."

"Who? I hope she was someone you liked!"

"Jemina . . . I—I liked her." Emily's mouth twisted into a tight line and a glint came into her eyes as if tears lay just below the surface. "But I shouldn't be talking about her. Father would be angry."

"Why? Didn't he like her?"

Emily looked down, hesitated, and sounded evasive "I'm surprised Father let you stay here . . . you look so much like her."

"You miss her? Can't you write or call?"

Emily never so much as raised her head and I could see by the way her eyes narrowed and her teeth pressed into her lower lip that she had been holding something back until she was ready to explode.

"Father never lets anyone mention her. Promise me you won't say anything to him about my mentioning her? Please!"

I patted her warm, pulsing hand, smiled "Word of honor."

Emily forced an uneasy smile "We're so isolated here. You're the first girl my own age I've spoken to in over a year. Father doesn't cotton to outsiders. People who aren't quite right— not true believers"

That startled me, but I couldn't think of any reply. It was just such an odd thing to say.

Emily settled into the big overstuffed wing-backed chair near the vanity. I pulled out the vanity's stool and we sat for awhile without talking. The long silence must have made Emily feel insecure again because the pink returned to her cheeks. I'd never met anyone so innocent and unsophisticated before.

But then my experiences with these odd isolationist sects had been limited to seeing them in the grocery and department stores. I wondered if all their daughters were this way. If so I might just go visiting them on my own. The lovely way the blush transformed her face made me laugh delightedly which only made her blush deepen more.

"Will you come down for breakfast?" she asked.

"If you want me to. Though I'm not very hungry. My head aches a little."

MR. ANDREWS AND EMILY'S SIBLINGS were already at the table. There must have been a dozen of the little ragamuffins—all boys unfortunately—it isn't that I hate boys. It's just that their frantic boisterousness was so . . . jarring. And this crowd was no exception. They kept jostling each other—and me—until Mr. Andrews intervened. They just seemed to be everywhere at once, reaching in every which direction, touching everything at the table. Back when I enjoyed such food it would have stolen my appetite to have dirty little boy hands handling every biscuit on a platter before deciding which one they wanted.

"How do you like your eggs, Melissa?" Mrs. Lafontaine asked, carrying in a platter of fresh biscuits.

"I'm sorry, Mrs. Lafontaine," I said, "but I'm really not hungry today."

"Oh, but you must have something! You're much too thin, girl."

I shook my head. "No, really."

"Mrs. Lafontaine is right, young lady," interjected Mr. Andrews thoughtfully. "You must have something That Henrich girl—the gymnast—starved herself to death last year. And a nice little gymnast she was too. Even if they make them wear those revealing costumes."

"Perhaps a little tomato juice." I yielded with great reluctance.

"Has anybody seen Josiah?" Zacariah, the oldest of Emily's horde of younger brothers, interrupted. He was nearly fourteen and dark olive with thick black hair cropped at his shoulders. The complete opposite of both Emily and her father. I wondered where he got his looks. Probably the proverbial milkman Mama always referred to, when she was feeling gossipy.

"He's probably out Tom-Catting around," Mrs. Lafontaine remarked with distaste. "I swear! That cat is worse than the postman. 'Neither rain nor snow nor dark of night' keeps him from the ladies."

"That's enough!" Mr. Andrews interrupted sharply.

Mrs. Lafontaine changed the subject. "I finally met the two women who bought the old Simms place." Mrs. Lafontaine started picking up empty plates and dirty napkins as she prattled on. "That Joyce Strandwick is one of *those* women," she said, giving Mr. Andrews a look that was simply pregnant with meaning. "Her hair's in a crew cut, men's pants and shirt —I thought she was a man at first. . . . It's shameful, Joseph. Absolutely shameful!"

Mr. Andrews's eyes narrowed and his lips thinned. "Keep the boys out of the far south pastures. I don't want them getting exposed."

"The worst news, Joseph, is the Oregon initiate failed to pass."

Mr. Andrews scowled. "I expected it would. Hoped folks would have enough sense to vote for it. Folks are just too easily misled these days. Queers own the networks . . . propagandizing our youth." He folded his cloth napkin, laid it next to his plate and pushed angrily away from the table.

All the time he said this he stared at Emily. I couldn't help thinking that if looks were daggers he would be murdering her. All the color faded from Emily's face as I watched from the corner of my eyes, pretending to sip at my tomato juice.

"The good Lord saw fit to punish Sodom and Gomorra for their perversions! And all who practice them are subject to his law." He spat, and the intensity of his glare made Emily shrink in her chair.

At that moment I hated Mr. Andrews. I didn't know what was going on, but I really didn't need to—I just hated him. Only my old promise to Mama (which was wearing thin) and my uncertainty about how Emily would react kept me from showing Mr. Andrews exactly how I felt about him and all his narrow-minded stiff-necked kind.

"Well, what can you expect in the last days, Joseph?" Mrs. Lafontaine said with a deep sigh, "All we can do is hold ourselves apart and wait for the Rapturing."

My stomach tightened. How could Mama have been so heartless as to dump me with people like these? There would be a reckoning this time when Mama returned.

"Amen, Mary. Amen." He turned his gaze to me. "As no doubt your fine mother told you many times."

I nodded. "That's why we moved to Montana."

"Your mother's an unusually godly woman for times like these! I'm proud to have a woman like that for a neighbor. Handsome widow-woman like her ought to have a husband. No shame in remarrying. Just haven't found the right woman until now."

Was he hinting that he was interested in Mama? It certainly sounded like it. I wished Mama had decided to stay in Montana this winter just so Mr. Andrews could discover exactly what kind of woman she was!

WHEN I ASKED HIM ABOUT a key for my room later that day Mr. Andrews proved very understanding—he attributed my desire for a key to the 'natural needs of a god-fearing young lady to feel her virtue was safe in strange surroundings.' (What I think he really meant was that he had an extra key and it wouldn't make much difference if I had one too.) So when I returned to my room late that night, I locked the door, but I also wedged a chair tightly under the knob just in case.

There had been nothing at dinner that I could eat since Mama and I have such unique dietary habits, but I picked at my food to avoid controversy. Then I slipped out of the house while they slept and went foraging up the road in Twin Springs. I came upon one of those isolated gas stations with the owner's home behind it that dot the rural highways. From the snowmobile tracks, frozen over and partially filled in, I saw that someone had left and not yet returned. I persuaded the lock to open and entered through the front door and up the stairs. I peeked into each room: three little girls slept in one and two young boys in another. The main bedroom beckoned to me and I entered. A young woman, not yet thirty, with a fine-boned, almost beautiful face woke suddenly as I entered. She sat up, dragging a big, gleaming gun from under her pillow.

Our eyes met and she hesitated. She raised the gun sluggishly, trying to hold it steady. "I'm a dream, my sweet one," I murmured persuasively, compelling her to look deeper into my eyes.

The woman made a last small effort to resist me, but all that she could manage was to twitch her shoulders as if to pull back. My gaze imprisoned her mind and soul as securely as if they were chains. The hand which held the gun slid down the side of the bed and hung strengthlessly. It was only a matter of moments before the weapon's weight would force it to fall from her grip to the floor. But I felt impatient. So I sat down beside her, pulled the gun from nerveless fingers and tossed it aside.

The woman whimpered low as I stroked her dark hair, kissed the pulse points in her throat and opened her nightgown. I slid my hand around her round ample breasts. Her nipples grew hard beneath my touch as I lifted her left breast to my lips. Then her whimpers became moaning as my fangs broke the full, ripe skin and I drank the sweet, tingling nectar within.

THE NEXT MORNING EMILY arrived early with a book under her arm. She was enveloped in an ankle length wool skirt and a loose, almost shapeless, sweater as protection against the frigid Montana winter. She came and stood behind me as I sat at the dressing table, brushing my long reddish chestnut hair. Emily reached out and covered my hand, stopping the brush.

"Let me do that," she said softly. "And I'll help you pin it up. Father thinks women who wear their hair down are wanton. He believes the sight of a woman's hair hanging down incited men to lust."

"That's crazy, Emily!"

She stroked my hair as she brushed it, smoothing the tangles into a flawless, burnished sheen. I could see the thoughtful frown on her face reflected in the dressing table mirror.

"I think so too." She said with a firmness that bordered on defiance.

"I suppose that's why I've seen you wearing skirts in the snow. Most girls I know you couldn't pry them out of their jeans once the weather got cold. Or any other time for that matter."

"Wearing pants usurps the authority that God granted to men." I could tell she was quoting her father by the stiffness of her words and the way she said them.

"Oh shit!" I rolled my eyes to the ceiling. "Well, I guess I'll have to find a way into town for a new wardrobe. I've got more jeans than dresses! Can't have the household in an uproar."

Then Emily did something that, considering all the care she had lavished on my hair, I never expected: She pulled and twisted it into a tight unattractive knot like her own and Mrs. Lafontaine's. However, I said nothing, figuring it was another one of those interminable "don'ts" that dominated life here.

Emily smiled. "Come on, get dressed and lets go outside. Mrs. Lafontaine has fixed us a basket lunch."

"No, silly!" Emily laughed. It suddenly occurred to me that in the day and a half I had never heard her laugh. All the other girls I have known her age laughed frequently. Some were even—Goddess forefend!—giggle-maniacs! But Emily was so serious she was almost somber. This was such a pleasant change.

"A picnic, yes. But not in the snow!" she said, moving to stand impatiently at the door, arms folded, an expression of deliberate mysteriousness on her face.

I put on a long wool skirt borrowed from Emily and, partly out of defiance wore my jeans underneath. While subzero temperatures didn't—as a rule do me any harm, I much preferred to be warm.

I carried the basket and Emily carried her book as we crossed the wide yard toward the barns. A thin layer of ice crusted snow crunched under our boots. I wasn't enthused about a picnic in a barn—I love horses and critters as much as any expatriate city girl can learn to, but don't want to eat with them.

To my relief Emily rounded the barn and I saw for the first time a wondrous sight: a magnificent greenhouse! My midnight expedition had carried me away from the barn, not toward it. Otherwise I would have seen this the night before.

It was like walking into permanent summer. It was warm and humid, but not unpleasantly so. Here everything was hydroponics and grow-lights. The outer rooms along the glassite panels were filled with fruit trees set in tremendous pots that bore year round: apples, oranges, lemons and limes, and most wondrously cherries. There were tomato vines heavy with fruit and bell pepper vines so lush with green, red and yellow peppers they looked like wax fruit. And there were isles of potatoes and other root crops in deep beds. No wonder Mr. Andrews, went into town so seldom! The ranch was practically self-sufficient.

There was a middle hall that ran the length of the greenhouse through a series of doors and chambers. Emily led me to a small door at the back of the greenhouse. Carefully stenciled on the door were the words: "EMILY'S ROOM."

"My fourteenth birthday present," she said with sudden blushing embarrassment. "Father isn't as harsh as he seems."

She opened the door and led me into a virtual fantasy land of lush ferns. I fell in love with it instantly.

"Sit down," she said, indicating a delicate French Provincial tea table and chairs."

"It's so beautiful, Emily!" I said settling the basket on the table. I turned and hugged her impulsively. But she winced and moved away.

Then I saw the tears running down her cheeks, she bit her lip, trying not to cry.

I put my hand out helplessly, "Emily, dear Emily, I am sorry. I didn't mean to upset you."

I reached out to touch her again and she flinched away. "Please don't."

A terrible suspicion hit me. Before she could move I had both her hands prisoned in mine and I had pulled up her sweater and blouse.

Long wide angry welts—the kind that a belt or an old fashioned razor strap leaves—ran across her flawless white skin. The edges were crusted with blood.

Mrs. Lafontaine's picnic in the green house idea must have been an attempt to comfort the girl and get her away from her father for awhile. Better to die than to live a life like hers.

Em—suddenly she wasn't Emily anymore, but someone else, someone I was falling madly in love with—had curled up in a little fetal ball, weeping brokenly, her face flushed with humiliation.

"Your father?"

"Yes," she said so softly even my sharp hearing could barely make it out.

"Does this kind of thing happen often?"

"Not often . . . Well . . . more often since I" she hesitated. "since I started developing. He says I'm like my mother. He found me . . . I borrowed a pair of your jeans," her voice came up just a little, almost a whisper now. "You weren't there— and a blouse. The crimson one with the—"

"Plunging neck line?" I supplied. It was my "fuck me" blouse. I only wore it for those special occasions. I could imagine her father's reaction to that combination! "And your hair was down?"

Em nodded. "Father caught me trying them on. I was looking at myself in front of the mirror. He didn't knock." Her voice was still soft but no longer a whisper. "He called me a harlot —like my mother."

Tears were starting in my own eyes as I got up and wedged the chair back under the door knob, then came back to Em stroking her brow. "It's going to be all right, Em. I'll make it all better." And Hell be damned if I let him hurt her again! I released her blonde hair, stroking it. I kissed away her tears, pressed my lips to her forehead. The warm humanness of her set me tingling.

Then I leaned over her tear streaked face, stared into her eyes and willed the pain away. I looked deeper and deeper, drawing her awareness in until nothing existed but the depths of our eyes—the mirrors of our souls. I hadn't Mama's subtlety and skills. But I couldn't bear to let Em hurt and had to reach deeply to block off the pain.

Em heaved a trembling sigh and relaxed.

As I started to sit back, Em impulsively pulled me to her and kissed me on the mouth—her tongue sought mine in a long hungry plunge.

Then I knew, for the first time in a long life, that I had met someone I couldn't continue without. And it frightened me. I knew that if I could not control myself, our love meant that Emily would die. Of course, I could bring her into the family. But that would make Mama so furious that I winced to think about it. And Mama was right sometimes: some people could handle it and others could not.

"I love you, Em." I whispered into her ear.

"I know. I love you too, Missy." Em smiled up at me with such adoration I wanted to cry.

I kissed her fingers and started up her hand to her wrist, but when I felt the pulsing of the vein in her wrist I felt suddenly dizzy and ravenous. I released her hand, tears of longing and frustration in my eyes. I stood and turned away.

"Missy! Come back. I love you."

"You don't know what you're asking, Em. You don't know."

"Don't you love me?"

"More than anyone I've ever loved before."

"Then make love to me, Missy."

"Em, I can't. My ways are death."

"I don't understand."

"I don't want you to."

That night I visited the young woman at the gas station again, but I left feeling unsatisfied and strangely empty.

JANRAE FRANK

"AREN'T YOU TWO SPENDING an awful lot of time out in the greenhouse?" Mr. Andrews inquired, buttering a piece of toast.

"It's so beautiful out there!" I said, pressing my gaze into his. After a moment he broke the glance and looked.

That worried me. Some people were resistant to me, especially men.

"Oh, Joseph," Mrs. Lafontaine chided him gently. "I gave them permission to do their studies out there after we finish in the mornings."

"And do they finish?" He demanded sharply

"Yes, of course!" she replied, "And if anything Missy is a good influence. Emily's showing a steady improvement in her composition and math."

"I'm not certain the greenhouse is healthy. There's an outbreak of some kind of anemia. Six cases in the last week."

"They were all at the edges of town," Mrs. Lafontaine pointed out. "They were exposed to it, if you ask me."

"Maybe I should cancel the girls shopping trip," Mr. Andrews said thoughtfully.

I saw the disappointment flit across Em's face and vanish. She was as good at hiding her feelings from her father as the proverbial Japanese.

"Nonsense! None of the afflicted were good Christian households!"

That depends on your definition of Christianity, I thought smugly.

"True. None of the Brethren have been touched by it."

So the shopping trip wasn't canceled.

MR. ANDREWS TOOK US into town in his snowmobile to shop as a special treat. Mama had sent me a letter and a large sum of cash. I offered half of it to Mr. Andrews to cover my room and board and he refused it, saying I was no trouble at all and he would feel insulted if I insisted. He also made it plain that he didn't take money from women. An archaic attitude, but I didn't feel inclined to argue.

It was a warm day for a Montana winter, a full 20 degrees warm. A wall of snow piled onto the sidewalks by the snow plows often forced us to walk in the streets. There were a few cars and an occasional snowmobile. But the stores were open and many of the owners had swept the walks clear enough for customers to find their way inside.

Whenever we could find a cleared sidewalk Em and I stepped onto it, feeling safer despite the infrequent automobile traffic. We stopped for a minute and watched a big truck go by salting down the plowed streets. It reminded me of upstate New York when Mama and I were living there a few decades ago. It doesn't seem that long at all! I smiled at the sweetness of the memory.

Just then we heard a loud continual honking begin. A procession of long, dark cars—with their headlights on in midday and black flags draped on their hoods—began passing by.

"Oh God! Make them stop!" Emily cried.

I turned and saw her half-bent over with her hands to her ears.

"Em?" I was stunned.

The cars continued to steer past us, their horns, becoming a hammering cacophony that clearly frightened Em.

"I hate funerals! I hate them!"

She twisted away from me when I reached for her. I frowned. "Em, its just a funeral."

"It depresses me. They had a funeral like this when my mother died. I didn't want to go but my father made me. Then he beat me later for throwing up when he made me kiss her body. They are burying Mrs. Bennett. She died a few days ago. It was all so sudden! Now two more women are showing symptoms. Father says it's AIDS breaking out again because there's so much sin in this town."

"Shhh," I soothed. "That's nonsense. Please, Em, I don't like seeing you so upset."

Em shook her head, sighing sadly. "I can't help thinking how tragic it is. She was so young. So was my mother. I often wonder if I'll die young too?"

"Come on, Em." I took her gently by the arm. "Let's go inside the yardage shop and look for some patterns and material. It won't be as loud inside."

"Why does everyone have to die?" She threw her arms around me in the street.

"Shhh! Stop talking about it and in a minute you'll stop thinking about it." I disengaged though I wanted to kiss her fears away.

"I don't want to die!" She repeated, her eyes closed and welling with tears.

"No one does, Em," I said gently.

Then I pulled her inside the shop where she slowly regained her composure as we examined the fabrics and patterns.

FOR THE REST OF THE DAY all I could think of was Em, her pale, white skin, the sweet throbbing of the pulses in her veins. I felt as if night would never come and when it did I felt as if it would never be bedtime. But eventually the household slept. Mortals are such fragile things and yet I am forever falling in love with them. I have loved many times, and yet I never loved as deeply as I loved Em.

My body melted into mist away at the thought of her

sleeping in the next room and I flowed to her under the locked door of my chamber.

Gathering myself at the foot of Em's old-fashioned brass bed I watched her breasts rise and fall with each breath. I hesitated, longingly, beside her. "Em, sweet Em," I murmured as I leaned over the bed, nuzzling the cleft between her white snowy mounds. Her bodice came loose and my lips moved down. Em moaned but did not wake.

*Em, Em, Em, goddess how I love you!* Her life essence welled to my lips like ambrosia of paradise.

She moaned and writhed beneath the sheets. A floorboard creaked outside. Em woke instantly as if at a bad memory and screamed. I vanished, misting away and back to my room.

"IT WAS A NIGHTMARE. Nothing more," Mrs. Lafontaine assured Em as the household crowded at her door.

I pushed past Em's younger sibling crowded at the door. Mr. Andrews stood near his daughter's bed, looking troubled. Mrs. Lafontaine sat on Em's bed, holding her while she sobbed and gasped and sobbed again.

"Is Emily all right?"

"She's had a nightmare," Mrs. Lafontaine said.

Em flushed and settled back into her pillows. "Oh. I'm sorry I woke everyone. Really." She caught at my hand as I moved away from the bed, "Sit with me until I fall asleep."

"I don't know," Mr. Andrews frowned.

"Oh, surely there's no harm in it," said Mrs. Lafontaine. Mr. Andrews shrugged.

I drew a chair near the bed and sat down.

Em watched the door close, then turned her lovely blue eyes to me, with an insistent, pregnant look. "Kiss me again like before, Missy. I won't scream this time. I promise."

I was startled and rose from my chair. "Em! What are you saying!"

"Oh, I don't know how . . . but I know." She looked away. "I've read books. I know what you are. Kiss me like that again, Missy."

"You don't know what you're asking." I moved to the window, gripping the ledge so hard my knuckles whitened.

"I do too," Her eyes met mine unafraid. "I'll never die, not really, and we can be together forever . . ." She halted and her eyes filled with tears "Unless you don't love me?"

"Dearest Em. Of course, I love you." I returned to the bed.

"Then kiss me again. Any life is better than this living death."

It was an inescapable truth. Em had won and I had lost. I bent over her, pressing my lips to the great blue vein in her breast.

To Hell with my promise to Mama. She would have to do the accepting, for once.

Finally I couldn't stand it any longer. As I lifted my blood-rimmed mouth from her delicate breast, Em moaning weakly beneath me, I could feel her dying. "No, Em. You mustn't leave me. Do you truly love me, Em?"

Her eyes, glazed with weakness stared up trustingly "Forever, Missy."

With a sharp fingernail I slashed my left breast and pressed her mouth to it. The blood flowed unheeded across her lips and for a moment I feared I had acted too late. Then I felt her sucking, weakly at first, then more strongly. "Yes, Em. Yes, yes, yes. Drink, Em, my love. Drink."

Suddenly the door slammed open with such force that the knob shattered against the wall. Mr. Andrews confronted us, a large black gun in his hand. My back had been to him. He had not seen what we had been doing, only our embrace.

I turned to move between Em and her father.

A normal woman would probably have felt vulnerable standing there in only a nightgown in front of a man with a loaded gun. I didn't.

"I thought so. You filthy pervert! I have been watching you." He gestured at me with his gun. "Now get away from my daughter."

"No," I said simply and stared at him, my lips drawing slowly, almost instinctively from my teeth.

"Please, father, don't!" Em cried in panic.

From the timber of her voice I could tell her strength was returning, and took heart. "Don't beg this time, Em." I said softly. "Not ever again!"

"I knew it! I knew it all along." He gritted the words with such hate that my soul shriveled. "You lesbian bitch! Seducing my child! Leading her in the path of sin and corruption!"

"Oh, I'm a lesbian all right." I said coolly, sauntering leisurely toward him. "But I'm also something more." I paused about two yards from Mr. Andrews, regarding him for a moment with my hands on my hips, then started forward again.

A hint of puzzlement came into his hard righteous expression. His finger tightened on the trigger. "Stand where you are, Miss Karnstein!" He ordered roughly.

I ignored him.

He still wasn't frightened when he fired. My body shuddered at the impact, but I felt no pain.

Even then he didn't get it. These fundamentalists! They claim they believe in the devil and the supernatural—but when they come face to face with them, none of them can ever truly believe it.

Mr. Andrews fired again. But I kept moving closer.

It was when the third shot failed to stop me that he panicked and emptied the gun. But by that point he was shaking so bad he only hit me once more. The wounds closed within seconds.

"Jesus Christ in Heaven save me!"

He stumbled backwards, fell, got to his knees, began to pray. His kind don't believe in crossing themselves or wearing crucifixes. The bible is enough for them—but it's damned inconvenient to carry as protection against the undead. Besides, holy objects only work for those whose actions are loving and godly. That left Mr. Andrews out.

I reached him before he could regain his feet and stood over him.

The empty gun trembled in his hand. His face was a mixture of hatred, fear, disbelief, and that look of simplicity that often precedes madness. I took the gun from him and crushed it. Then he began the Lord's Prayer in a fractured fashion, unable to finish it before he gave up and started over.

"If there's a heaven, Mr. Andrews, I wouldn't count on your getting there." My hand closed on his throat and I lifted him off the ground. He strangled in my grasp. Yet that look of mindless hate and loathing—not of my state as one of the undead—but for my loving his daughter—never faltered.

After a time his struggles grew weaker, ceased entirely. I dropped him. I never once considered drinking from him, even the thought was distasteful. I mean he was sewer water compared to Em's champaign.

I felt Em's eyes on my back and I turned. "I'm sorry," I said.

"Don't be," she answered. There were tears in her eyes, but they were not for her father. "He imprisoned me. You released me. He caught me with Jemina when I was sixteen. We'd been lovers for two years. That's why we're in Montana . . . But . . . but," her voice started to shake a little, "I heard Mrs. Lafontaine say Jemina disappeared just before we moved. I don't think she ran away. I think father—" she didn't finish.

I could hear the rest of the house stirring in response to the shots and grabbed Em's hand. "Let's go," I said. "I'll show you how."

She looked at me trustingly, grasping my hand tighter as I drew her to the window. "Take a deep breath," I told her, staring deep into her eyes. "Then imagine yourself melting into mist."

She did and we flowed out over the snow, leaving not the slightest footprint behind.

Maybe this was what they meant by Happy Ever After. I hoped so. But only the centuries will tell.

# Two-Spirits

## CHRIS MORAN

*Most people search for the meaning of life; her search was a little different.*

I.

OMMON SENSE is something I really don't have much of anymore, not *much*.

Mark's body folded onto the floor in a sad, twisted pile of bone and leather after . . . after *I tried to bring him <u>with</u> me.* I tried, but I couldn't find the *essense,* the seed—that sweet, sweet, pindot of primordial juice that you can find when you draw on a human . . . and you draw, and you draw, and you draw out all the banalities, all the laundry lists, all the forgotten dinners, all the blind dates, all the jobs at Chicken-Jerk-To-Go. And then . . . sometimes, only sometimes . . . you find it: The sweet human being-ness, the love of animals and leaves and water and soil; the wonderment of the moon; the awe of women's courage and fertility, of men's tenacity, of their *audacity.*

But, no. What I found was all that Mark really desired in his deepest heart-of-hearts was a Masarati and a cheap fling with a drag queen on a muggy Saturday night. A shallow, loveless husk whose promotion from six boring years as an associate with Lautman, Kirk, and Dunn had nothing more to offer him but an extra zero to his holy goddamn bank account, a dimestore stock portfolio, and an unlimited credit line at Nordstrom's.

And then, I saw that I was the drag queen to be had on a muggy Saturday night, to be momentarily adored, to be briefly fondled, to be . . . a *cheap* drag queen at that. . . .

So I kept on sucking.

Then, there was nothing to be kept pure, nothing, except the simple fact of his birth. And even that was suspect in my book. Certainly nothing to be kept alive . . . at least alive *forever*. He almost had me sold with his sweet, pseudo-cosmic tenderness when he ticked off that box on the back of his driver's licence which would someday donate his sorry, diseased liver to the Children's Cancer Society. He almost sold me again when he recited a long, dewy, politically correct diatribe about the plight of pre-adolescent, organic coffee pickers in El Salvador. But, all that is past now.

Now, like a complete idiot, I've dialed 911 and I'm sitting in this little rathole of a hotel room, three blocks north of the Greyhound, waiting for an ambulance to show up. Probably the cops and the coroner, too—because all I really want is to be done with it. *All* of it. All one hundred and fifty-three years of it. And I have no fucking idea what I'll tell them when they show, when the black-and-white rattles to a stop below my window, spewing out its salt-and-pepper crime-fighting team of pure compassion and empathy. No fucking idea of what iron-clad alibi or judicious reason I'll offer to them for this cold-blooded, and it was *cold*-blooded, extermination—"Officer, I just couldn't stand this fuckin' greedy, creep anymore, so I just sucked out every fuckin' ounce of his precious fuckin' life's juices and the goddamn asshole just fuckin' died on me. . . ."

No, that won't work.

I'll just do what I've done many times before. Many more

times than I'd care to admit. I'll just slip out at the last minute, vanish. There will be no clothes, no knickknacks, no finger-prints, no combs with tangled hairs, no lipstick smeared tissues, no traces. The hotel cashier won't be able to read my name on the register. He won't be able to tell them what I looked like, what I sounded like, what I wore, what fabulous three-day old essense I smelled of. My entire being will become tantalizingly elusive tidbits afloat on his pale, watery memory. Gone. Done. Good bye.

No, no common sense at all.

## I I.

*A DEEP, ALMOST BOTTOMLESS bluish-green is the color I always see when I dream of the Gila Mountains. I've never seen another color like it. Nowhere else in New Mexico, cer-tainly nowhere east, nor west, at least not on land. A color that to this day, even in the midst of this rancid afterthought called Los Angeles, I still find piercing. Maybe it was the reddish-orange clay of the flayed hillsides against the dark juniper and pine. Maybe just the way the light settled along the Mogollon Rim at dusk. But that color, that heartbreaking shade of color resonated through me, far beneath my skin.*

*It was in that cast I first saw Jonathan. I was sick with the smell of silver wafting off the mine tailings in the late afternoon winds. Except for a half plate of beans and a couple of stale tortillas negotiated from the livery helps' breakfast, I hadn't eaten all day, unless you'd call miners' coffee and roll-your-owns food. But at that moment my dizzy, aching head didn't matter, the vacant condition of my belly didn't matter. What mattered was the single, singular image in front of me.*

*On the boardwalk across from General Dry Goods, I was*

*trying to sweep up enough courage to walk into the tavern for a short, but numbing shot of gin. It was all I needed to set my spirit for a night of work. At nineteen, and looking fifteen, it took more than just a little courage to just* open *the tavern door, since I had been with a good third of the miners in town, and both barkeeps, and I hadn't been resident in Mogollon more than four months. Bragging rights notwithstanding, I was frozen short in my steps by the sight of what appeared to be a white man, at least six-foot-four with long dark hair, wearing a doeskin shirt, black breeches, and dismounting from a mottled-gray Appaloosa mare.*

*Even in that wild part of the country he was impressive. I wasn't the only one who paused to take note, but I was definitely the longest, most gaping to take note. A lot of men in mining country let their hair grow for a time, eventually succumbing to some local Russian or Chinese barber so as not to be mistaken for an Indian, or "half-breed," or worse. Worse being that type who wound up sleeping with the top of the pecking order amongst the miners, that is, if he was young looking enough.*

*Naturally, I had the experience to know.*

*But what struck me as unusual wasn't the man's hair, or his mount, or even his size, but the fact that he wore doeskin. Most men, whether they were Indian or white, wore the tougher yellow-tanned buckskin, even in summer. Doe was usually only worn by Indian children, women and, strange to me then, "medicine men."*

*And while I tried to collect my jaw and tongue and bulging eyes into some expression of dignity and discretion, the man-in-doeskin paused, and taking his saddlebags down from his mount, turned and stared straight in my direction as if I had called out to him by name. His eyes burned right into the back of my eyes. Whatever thoughts were trying to line themselves* up in my young brain at that moment, all-at-once, shook loose with a violence, my ankles wobbled and I had to steady myself against the veranda post.

So much for dignity. So much for discretion.

The man-in-doeskin hiked his satchels over his shoulder and then did the unthinkable: He walked towards me. In a focused, even gait, he walked across the dusty, pot-holed street, towards me.

His boot heels creaked on the veranda steps. "Find decent food in there?" he asked, nodding at the tavern door.

What I found was that the scuff marks on the toes of my shoes might reveal the secrets of eternity if I stared at them long enough. "Jack Spence b-bagged a mule deer this morning . . . M-may be stew," I stammered.

"Good. Join me inside?"

Somehow, I managed to ratchet my neck in the direction of his voice, meeting his eyes from below my hat brim. ". . . Sure . . . maybe-in-a-bit." My stomach betrayed my nonchalance with a growl.

The man-in-doeskin nodded. His eyes burned a clear blue flame. I returned to the toes of my shoes. He opened the tavern door to a wave of sodden noise and tobacco smoke mixed with the smell of grilling meat.

I turned slightly to study him out of the corner of my eyes: the pitch of his shoulders, the shape of his thighs, the worn patina on the shafts of his boots. The man-in-doeskin spent a lot of time on horseback.

The tavern door closed soundlessly behind him.

Gin could wait. Food could wait. The miners could definitely wait. My mind was the consistency of poached tripe. After I found my legs and pulled my eyes back into focus, I set off across the street to the dry goods store and planted myself near

the man-in-doeskin's Appaloosa, deciding to just sit and watch
. . . and wait.

The tavern door must have opened fifty times over the next
two hours. It gave up every conceivable brand of humanity
known to the New Mexico Territory: Spanish, English, Chinese,
Russian, one-legged, two-legged, miners, thieves, bankers,
hucksters, lawyers, drifters, the odd Indian, the more odd
woman, the dead sober, the dead drunk. The man-in-doeskin
was not among them.

I retreated and collapsed back into the end stall at the livery.
The help there were buried in a card game and a bottle of cheap
whisky in the loft. After the smell of the miners, the smell of
stabled horses was as welcoming as lilac water. Bursts of
outrage and laughter poured down upon me from the loft, yet I
fell asleep on the spikey, three-day old straw as if someone
had clubbed me from behind.

I could have been asleep for three minutes, or three hours,
or three days.

The wet fog of the Appaloosa's breath and the nutty smell of
her muzzle coaxed me from dead sleep to soupy consciousness. What I could make out in the dim lantern light was the
shape of a man cinching the saddle of my new, nuzzling
stablemate. I didn't move. The man-in-doeskin stood over me,
studying me. Any other time I would have been terrified, or
lashing out, or most likely, both. Instead, I felt reassured, calm,
peaceful, accepting . . . wanting.

"We can't stay here through the night. We must leave." His
eyes flashed in the lantern light.

We, I thought? I couldn't even raise a stutter. My head cocked.

"I have no more purpose here," he answered, " and you are
not safe."

Even though I knew how true this was, his pronouncement

*soured me with resentment. How would he know anything about my life? I coughed to find my voice.*

*"The Mescaleros will raid Mogollon before week's end. This town of money and grief will burn." His voice sounded strange, foreboding, foreign.*

*I struggled to respond to him. Laying back on the straw, I felt dizzy, sick to my stomach, and managed to bubble some words about my knapsack and my hat.*

*Another eternity later I awakened on horseback to a sharp jolt, my hands loosely lashed around the man-in-doeskin's waist. We came to a slow halt. "She's usually surefooted . . . even on creekbeds . . . Do you need to get down?" He untied the lashings.*

*I slipped off the mare and stood groggily at the edge of the trail to piss.*

*Running away would have been easy. My gut told me that the man-in-doeskin wouldn't try to stop me. Silver Creek would lead me back to town in little more than a day by foot. But what would I have returned to? The bugridden mattresses of the miners' camps? Stealing pinches of gold dust in the cold pre-dawn just to afford a cheap muslin shirt, or a leather-tough shank of horse meat or mule? The bitter ridicule of the "god-fearing and respectable" wives of the mine owners and bankers who sold themselves nightly to the thieves and robbers who were their husbands?*

*I wanted to reel around and demand the man-in-doeskin's name and where he was from and why he was doing what he was doing—to stamp the dirt to protest his taking me from Mogollon without so much as a whisper of my permission, and shout at him for tying me so intimately to his body. By what right, I wanted to ask? By what right? And . . . and . . . I was utterly and completely mute . . . filled with a rare calm.*

*Calm and* awe.

*We rode down through the gentle corridors of cottonwood and sycamore which lined Silver Creek towards Glenwood. I watched crested blue jays swoop and squawk at our intrusion. Purple lupine and brilliant, red firepoppies danced hypnotically in the steady breeze. Tiny mountain finches skidded from tree limb to bush to tree limb, engaged in their incomprehensible gossip. Sunlight glowed through the branches.*

### III.

I WON'T WORRY YOU with all the usual, *how* lonely it is, *how* tiring it can be, *how* boring it can get—oh, yeah, *and* how glamorous and how exciting and how full of intrigue and passion; and, you know, the mysteries of the dark, the cruel knowledge of the light, and so on, and so on, and so on, and . . . five generations worth, five fucking *lives* worth. Girlfriends, boyfriends, husbands, confidantes, partners, bosses, bartenders, blacksmiths, drugstore clerks, plumbers. I mean, it gets to the point, and a rather depressing point at that, you basically see most people as one of two things:

Enemies or food.

And the rest of world just kind of falls into rank.

But that's only part of the formula, loved-ones. There are enemies, there is food, and then, there are . . . doctors.

You see, as much as I would love to claim the holy powers of transfiguration and magically appear to you as the whole and complete image of "Woman" which I have so ardently dreamed of within my flat, boyish chest—the body I was born with is, very sadly, the one I've got forever. For*ever.*

If I had been born with webbed hands or stunted legs, or a headless, withered Siamese-twin skewed to my belly, or some such other known misfortune of disheveled physiology, you might feel at the very least, some desolate, twinging pang of sympathy for me. But for that boyish flat chest and the very man-sized phallus that's stuffed beneath my crotch to be claimed as my great and lonely bodily grief?

How many male children are born to this planet so well-endowed with health and life and, and . . . such great membership? Shouldn't I be just a little bit grateful to be so gratefully blessed? Or, how many *women*, raped, beaten, burned, cast aside, trapped within the suffocating confines of their gender, who without much more than a second thought, if not a third, would gladly give up their wombs and teats to enjoy the born privileges of men?

And I should be different?

Yes. But tiresomely yes, achingly *yes, fucking* yes, for that matter. I've been after a good sex doctor for the past sixty-some years, sixty-some *odd* years since I read about Einar Wegener trying to get a womb transplant in Denmark so he, and I mean "he" very thinly, could become Lille Elbe. And the sob story *there,* sisters and brothers, was that she, *she,* died a few days after her final operation, her promised future as a *new* woman lost forever. But at the very least, she had those few days, those handfuls of precious hours to, dare I say it, realize her peace. Her outside finally looked like, felt like her inside, and when she awakened those few mornings, she did not awaken to some strange, hard alien body, but . . .

But trying to find a doctor to work on *me?* The examination always stops about the time the poor nurse tries to find my blood pressure. Only the Holiest of Holies knows what she would find next! Just too much explaining to do . . . *You see, sweetheart, I don't have what you'd call blood pressure . . . Do I have a pulse? . . . Pulse. Is that the same as circulation?*

*Hmmm, well, I do breathe, would you like to check my breathing? You see* . . . and then, well, her mind starts getting cloudy, the doctor's memory goes vague (no surprise there, at least), the receptionist suffers a profound lapse of recall, and I'm gone . . . done . . . good-bye. Once, again.

It's not like I haven't tried to *explain* it to a doctor before. Doctors are used to the out-of-common, the unusual, the strange, if you will. A person with a seemingly male body wanting to have a seemingly female body? What? No problem? Just three hundred hours of senseless psychiatric screenings, a grubstake in the pharmaceutical hormone industry and about twenty grand to drop into a surgeon's personal retirement account. Then all that awaits is snip, snip, snip and sew, sew, sew . . . No, no problem at all! Until, that is, I get to the place where I start explaining what he will eventually find in his physical examinations, like how my metabolism has slowed to something akin to a granite boulder or a Galapagos tortoise— not to *mention* my most essential nutritional needs. And when his staunch disbelief is gradually replaced by wide-eyed, bulging terror and his immediate response changes from calling the little men in white suits to calling the big men in blue suits . . . well, then I only have *one* choice: Lunch. And at that point, sweet ones, it's justice, pure and simple. Justice.

One might suppose, at four o'clock in the morning, sitting in this dirty little downtown pocket of stink with a dead, barely identifiable human body lying at my feet, that I may have become jaded, even cynical. That the Gift given to me those five generations ago was a shameful waste. The thought *has* crossed my mind.

But shame has not been a foreign feeling in my lives.

And when the ceiling is about to collapse in upon me, when the earth threatens to open up and swallow me wholly and vengefully, when the very air turns to smothering mud—then my reaction is to sit, just sit, light a Viceroy, study the cracked paint on the windowsill, cross my legs, stare at the buzzing cafe sign across the street . . . the blurs of pulsing blue light . . . listening to the sirens . . . dreaming . . .

In the distance, the sirens sound like sorry, mechanical imitations of coyotes—the coyotes who hung on the perimeters of our camps when even the hearty kangaroo mice and spotted lizards couldn't survive the drought.

The air was thick with dry, gray dust. Sometimes a whelping bitch would slowly zig-zag her sagging, hunched frame towards our fire, begging food.

The proud, wild coyote was not above shame, if it meant life.

### IV.

*THE MAN-IN-DOESKIN didn't speak another word to me until dusk when we reached a craggy, dark ravine which forked wildly off of the creek canyon. Fifteen minutes up the ravine we came to a large outcropping of purple rock—beneath which lay an impossibly flat plane of hard, yellow clay maybe thirty feet wide by thirty deep. In the center of the perfect clay square was a large spiral of smooth black river stones, four long paces across, each stone almost identical to the next, each weighing about eight pounds. My jaw trembled at the sight of it. I slid off the side of the Appaloosa and stared.*

*"This is my dreaming ground," the man-in-doeskin said. "We can camp here for now. You'll be safe."*

*"Safe from what?" In the overwhelming strangeness of my new surroundings, I found my tongue, ". . . and who are you?"*

*"My name is Jonathan Rainbow," he replied "You'll be safe*

here, *that's all I can guarantee you right now.*

*"This is the place where I come to dream and pray," he made a reverent, sweeping gesture encompassing the expanse of the broad ravine. "This is the place where I first* saw *you—during my dreaming—and I knew through my dreaming that you needed my help."*

*"Your help? How can you help me?" Mistrust was an inborn quality of mine. "And what do your damned* dreams *have to do with me?"*

*"I know . . . you do not think that dreams mean anything— that the only ones you remember are your nightmares." He explained steadily. My heart seemed to slow a few hundred beats. "But dreams to me are another way of* seeing *a person, understanding a person . . . a place and a time. Then I know how to pray. Then I know what to do."*

*"I start there when I begin my dreaming," pointing to the center stone of the black spiral. "And then I go to there," his finger tracing the graceful curves to the end stone. "And then I go to* there," *Jonathan Rainbow, the man-in-doeskin, pointed directly to my heart, laughing until his generous brown eyes crinkled into a hundred tributaries of thin, dark crevices.*

*I was shocked at his familiarity and confused by his meanings, yet at the same time, comforted by his attention and his, at least apparent, attraction to me. I had been an object of desire and lust often during my young life, but expressions of genuine interest or affection? Those were as foreign as France.*

*"You were on the edge of death, dear one, one way or another," he recounted. "Either a hungry miner, or a woman jealous of your ways, or the Mescalero's revenge would have been your death. I saw this in my dreaming as right as you are now breathing. . . . No doubts. . . . None. But I also saw you as a worthy—and as a* worthy *you must come with me. That is*

*your destiny . . . not just my desire . . . maybe not your's either . . . just your destiny . . . and mine."*

He did not wait for another question. The man-in-doeskin quickly dismounted and walked across the clay, behind the stone circle to the back wall of the outcropping, laying his bedroll and saddlebags near a small black fire pit below the overhang of purple rock. Jonathan turned toward the wall and reached up into the shadows to unlatch a wooden meat-smoking crib suspended from the rock ceiling. He produced several strips of venison backstrap and layed them across a spit. The gamey smell brought me across the smooth clay floor with no second thought. By sight, the meat hadn't aged more than a couple of days. I stiffened and turned to face my "rescuer."

"So you think food will buy me?" I fired at him. "Shit, even old Banker Reagan didn't think of that one when he had me kidnapped as his whore!" My voice trailed off, ". . . Tried just about everything else. . . ."

Jonathan raised his palm quickly. "Eat if it suits you, then leave if it suits you. Take my mare. You choose."

I stared intently at the-man-in-doeskin for what seemed like hours. My eyes flooded in grief and confusion, my shoulders quaked, but I did not cry. All of the voices in my head had their say, all at once—the skeptics, the adventurers, the naysayers, and the rosy-cheeked Pollyannas—a full, discordant chorus of conflicting thoughts and feelings. And as deeply as I mined these jumbled inner voices—which, granted, kept me alive the past five years—I couldn't find the brilliant, unmistakable red flag of danger that would put me into immediate flight, a flight which I had travelled so breathlessly, but so gratefully, many times before.

Instead, the arguments between my head and heart silenced themselves like two drunken debaters in a bar at closing time.

*The feeling which enveloped my consciousness was that of a warm, but odd homecoming, akin to walking through the familiar, sunlit front door of my childhood home, but seeing the furniture rearranged on the ceiling. My knees slowly buckled my body into a sitting position. I lowered my eyes from Jonathan's gaze.*

*"I have no wish to use you," the man-in-doeskin responded to my thoughts. "Your's is not to take like a thief. Your's is not to take by me or anyone else . . . at least . . . that is, not simply." He laughed at his own ironies. My face flushed and the tears which I so stubbornly held behind my eyes, welled and poured over my cheeks. And at the same time, I smiled widely, and laughed with this complex and strange man-in-doeskin. Honesty was far too rare in my young experience not to be appreciated—and fully.*

*Jonathan rose, silently mouthing the word "firewood" to me and disappeared into the nearby brush. My eyes wandered along the yellow clay floor. One set of footprints led from the right flank of the Appaloosa to where I sat. My set. I could not see another. Jonathan had walked across the from the left. My eyes quickly followed what I knew to be his trail to the brush. No footprints. I could hear the sharp snaps of dry willow branches. Jonathan emerged a few moments later carrying a large bundle of gray tinder.*

*"We'll eat soon, then you can sleep," he pronounced.*

*"My name is Temple Doolin," I barely offered. He tipped his head slightly and smiled.*

*Jonathan lighted a fire and seared the spit of venison. "You are a Two-Spirit, a Man-Woman, eh?" He glanced up at me from the corners of his eyes. I stammered and looked away from him. "What the Chiracahua call* Mahoe *. . . The Lakota would call you* Winkteh. *The Dineh would call you* Nadleh.

CHRIS MORAN

*The whites don't have a respectful name for you. . . . There is no place in their world for those such as you. That is their misgiving."*

*I didn't know what all those strange names meant, but Jonathan's term "Man-Woman" was pretty unmistakable. My eyes widened with exposure and shame. I had run away from Chicago at fourteen after my father was sent home early form the stockyards, ill one Saturday, and payed a surprise visit to his three daughters and one son playing in the cramped backyard of their southside brownstone. What he discovered, however, was his <u>four</u> daughters playing in the cramped backyard of their southside brownstone. And in a brief moment, my mother's and sisters' fourteen years of secret, loving insulation from the real world unraveled in chaos. I escaped bruised, torn, exhausted and heartbroken the following Monday. "Man-Woman" and "Two-Spirit" were easily the nicest names thrown at me since.*

*Jonathan snapped his fingers above the fire pit. "You are blessed, but you see it as a curse!" His eyes riveted on mine, his voice became concentrated, intense. "<u>Blessed</u> with the power of both woman and man—not <u>cursed</u>! If you were born into the world of the red people, you would hold the office of ceremony, you would be called the mediator between women and men, between earth and sky, between the powers of death and life. You would be held in esteem and attend births and weddings and dyings. You would be wealthy."*

*Jonathan offered me a skewered length of blackened venison. My eyes did not leave his as I took it from him.*

*"But to live among <u>your</u> people, who long ago were my people too, you must* choose. *You cannot be both woman and man. No other path is made for you there. Your woman's soul will betray your man's body, or your man's body will betray your*

woman's soul. To live in their world you must choose between being a woman or a man. There is no other path for you there except that of struggle or . . . madness . . . or . . . sickness . . ."

I stretched to follow his frightening narrative while nervously trying to eat my fill of the welcome meat. My mind flooded with visions from my past which proved out the man-in-doeskin's dire warnings: The relentless singsong tauntings of my childhood schoolmates which evolved into near daily beatings as those gentle, delicate boy-children grew into rough and tumble youths, while I remained gentle and delicate or how, later, my fellow boxcar stowaways, convinced that I was a girl, tried to have their way with me and wound up pummeling me within an inch of my life when they discovered that my anatomy didn't meet their expectations—or in St. Louis when I was arrested and placed in a boys' home where I was made out to be the nightly amusement until I figured out that the front gate had no lock on it and I made an uneventful, indeed casual, broad daylight "escape" three months later. (I'm certain, to this very moment, that the dormitory masters just looked the other way while offering their sincere and devout prayers of thanks.)

In Tulsa, and two years later in Austin, I learned to ply my misfortunes in order to eat. Cattlemen and buckaroos were generous enough, but they were also skittish—not wanting to appear soft on young "boys" to their trailmates, I frequently suffered a swollen cheek or black-eye that took weeks to heal as I retreated to a backroom job washing dishes or scrubbing floors where my damage was hidden from view. Mogollon, though much smaller, was not much safer . . . but it was <u>still</u> a living . . .

Jonathan stopped speaking. I was lost in a fog. I attempted to refocus my eyes.

CHRIS MORAN

"*Hearing the truth will do this to a soul,*" *he grinned and stood up.*

"*In the red people's world, Two-Spirits are allowed to be complete,*" *he paced back and forth opposite me across the fire pit.* "*The men Two-Spirits may appear as women, but they may also join the warrior men. The Brave-Hearted Women may go to war as warriors and marry women, or they may weave, or cook, or marry men. Their paths are free.*

"*Osh-Tish, the Crow, wears dresses with the patterns of flowers, but he is also known as* Finds-Them-and-Kills-Them! *As both, your world only allows you to sell yourself to men's beds.*"

"*You're not Indian?*" *I asked exhaustedly.*

"*No. No, my people are older than the red people. My people are called the Old Keepers.*" *Jonathan replied in a slow, measured meter.* "*My people are not related by birth . . . but we are related by blood.*" *He paused.* "*I will wake you in the morning and we will talk then. . . .*"

*I sunk back onto my elbows, and then my shoulders. My fatigue penetrated to the center of my bones. The fire's heat drained me of any further resistance. My eyes fluttered closed. I felt the weight of a large animal skin tucked around my shoulders.*

*Then began an old familiar ritual which visited upon me every night since I left home.*

*My sleep was dreamless, like stone, always like stone. In the early morning hours, inextricably, like a dynamite blast, I startled awake, every inch of my body soaked in my own sweat. I did not know where I was and reeled about in my bedding. Lost, I gasped, and trying to claw my way out of the enveloping panic, felt something . . . someone . . . breathing . . . very close to me . . . very close, very deeply, very slowly, very measured* breathing. *My eyes emerged from the dark purple of night to see the man-in-doeskin, his huge body appearing to completely encircle mine, radiating an aura of peace and calm with every cavernous breath. Inhaling, exhaling, inhaling, exhaling. My breathing started to match his. My heart stopped racing. I started to relax and cautiously lowered myself back against his massive shoulder, slowly dropping back asleep . . . seemingly, for the first time in many years . . . safe asleep.*

## V.

THE WILD, SOUR HOWLS of ambulance and police sirens din as they approach the hotel. I'm almost out of cigarettes, staring at the wide, ragged run snaking down the stocking over my right shin. Fucking pantyhose. As in life, Mark was grasping, and *clawing* to the end.

I wonder if they'll keep me hush-hush as they did fortysome years ago with the "flying saucer" crash in Roswell, New Mexico, or when they discovered the alchemical diaries of the Compe de St. Germain before the Crash of '29? (Who knew making gold was *that* easy?)

No, these days I'll just become the star of the moment. Paraded through the tabloids, then "News at Six," then the innumerably ridiculous talk shows. Montel Williams would suit me just fine—*Exclusive: She-Male Vampire Talks!*, or *I Was A Cross-Dressing, Bloodsucking Murderer!* I can smell the headlines now.

But the sorry truth, soulmates, is that it doesn't really matter if I am a "vampire" or not. Neither does it matter if I am a "transsexual"—or not. Either way I am made out to be an outlaw. Either way I am some *thing* which looks wrong and vile to the rest of this world. Either way I live at least two separate lives, no matter how hard I try to pass myself off as "normal," as a mortal human or as a "vampire," as a "woman" or as a "man." Which lie do I tell today? *Just accept yourself, you say? Just be who you are,* you say? The glowing, androgynous child who glides through my memories? The bruised teenage whore who turns a trick in order to afford a lunch of boiled tongue? The budding, darkly hopeful "vampire" avenger of <u>all</u> the world's wrongs? The frustrated, raging, homicidal drag queen? *Two*-Spirit!? Try "*Three*-Spirit"! Try "*Four*-Spirit"! *Just accept yourself,* you say? *Just be who you are,* you say? Take your pick.

Then come on up and visit it me in my hotel room . . . sometime . . .

## VI.

*THE RISING SUN WARMED the damp, gray corners of the ravine. Two large black ravens briefly circled our camp, fighting, diving at each other, punctuating the air with their harsh, rasping calls. I watched Jonathan build another meat-smoking crib, while I pensively ate my breakfast of roasted corn and bitter tea. His disturbing words from the night before echoed inside of my head.*

*Jonathan looked up at me from his labor as if he heard my thoughts. "We are going up to the mesa this morning—maybe over to the next canyon . . . I want to show you how I hunt—that is, if you promise not to fall asleep on me," he laughed ironically. I feigned a smile and returned to denuding my corn cob.*

*There was little question in my mind of who I was, of who I knew myself to be—my body, however, didn't seem to agree with my final conclusions. And, then, even my body's answers were pretty vague. But the idea of choosing to be a man or a* woman? For nineteen years of age, my face was fair; my build slight, some would call frail; my stride graceful, and my voice an even-tempered alto. When I arrived outside of Tulsa, some three years ago, I noticed that strangers approached me with a curious deference, studying my body, maybe my walk, or the pitch of my voice; then hedged their bets that I was probably a girl dressed for farm work, as was common in rural parts. They most often treated me with the genteel social courtesies reserved for born females. I would rarely bother to correct them, but I also managed to make a quick retreat.

Yet, even if I were built like a growling lumberjack, the voices of my mind, my sight, my loves, my dislikes, my passions informed me that my soul was <u>different</u>, certainly not a man's soul, at least no man who I've ever met, but far, far more akin to a woman's soul. It just was. Exactly how it figured as such I may never really know. But there was never a matter of choice. There was nothing to prove or disprove to myself, or anyone else. It was simply a fact of my being alive, like breathing. On the other hand, attempting to live my life with some semblance of sanity between my woman's soul and my boy's body, that constant nagging, disappointing rift in the reality of my life, that was another matter entirely . . .

WE HIKED TO THE TOP of the mesa by mid-morning and positioned ourselves behind a blind of gray broom bush. Once there, Jonathan dabbed me with short strokes of cod-liver oil and then instructed me to breathe in eight distinct parts: Four short inhalations, four short exhalations. I felt foolish hiding in a bunch of bushes, wreaking of dead fish and breathing like a woodmouse. The deer, he instructed, sensed humans through sight, smell, and sound, particularly the sound of human respiration. Our sight was covered by the blind, our smell by *the oil, and the familiar rhythm of human respiration by our adopted pattern of breathing. According to him, a deer could pass six inches in front of us and never detect that a human was present. No doubt.*

*Jonathan then looked at me in complete earnest and said, "Now pray to the deer, to it's spirit, to come to us, to present himself to us so that we may hunt him." This may have been the strangest thing someone had ever asked me to do—that is, outside of choosing to be a man or a woman.. "Just pray," he emphasized. I closed my eyes and followed his lead. "Now thank the deer." I opened one eye and looked at Jonathan like a begging human question mark. "Do it," he commanded. I did.*

*I practiced breathing in, then out, four beats apiece. I repeated the pattern a hundred times. My head grew lighter. My sight fixed on the scintillating reflections of the leaves gently dancing in the breeze just a few inches from my face. A mockingbird recited her entire repertoire. I lost track of time.*

*The next sensation I felt was Jonathan's huge hand closing around my wrist, momentarily squeezing it to get my attention. A buck deer with four and five point antlers passed not more than three feet in front of us. Jonathan's eyes met mine. The message was unmistakable:* Don't move!

*Within an instant Jonathan leaped from the blind and enveloped the animal in his grasp. Amidst a violent flurry of dust and broken branches, I watched the drama as if I were seeing the event at half its speed. His hands moved quickly to immobilize the deer's antlers and jaw, while his legs scissored above animal's hindquarters and swept it's legs out from under it. Only then did I realize that Jonathan had no weapons with him. No rifle, no bow and arrow, no knife.*

*When the thick dust of their lightning-quick battle cleared, I beheld an image that fascinated and then terrified me: the buck* lay on the ground, twitching the last of life from its body. *Poised over the dying form, Jonathan firmly braced the deer's head and legs with his hands while his torso arched over it's back.*

*As I warily approached I could see Jonathan's face almost buried in the animal's broad neck, accompanied by a wild, horrific sucking sound. The twitching stopped. Jonathan's head rose from the dead animal's neck where appeared an apple-sized puckering reddish-purple hole. My eyes swelled in their sockets. Jonathan slowly lifted his face to the sun. His expression was of absolute peace and serenity. There was no trace of blood or flesh on his mouth. I looked back to the wound on the deer's neck and watched it close like the aperture of a camera lens, screwing itself into a dry, mottled scar. I felt a cold chill run through the marrow of my entire skeleton, my breathing constricted like a fist and my heart beat furiously. Jonathan opened his eyes, sensing my panic, yet not even he could react quickly enough to stop my wild scrambling body, which raced towards the edge of the mesa to the trail which would thankfully lead me back to camp, and some minuscule sense of the known and the familiar.*

*"Temple!" Jonathan shouted at me, "Temple Doolin!"—less than a dozen strides behind me. Without slowing my frantic escape, I turned to see him, and at the moment, felt my soul ripping hotly in two halves: One desperately fleeing from the life-sucking monster I envisaged just seconds earlier, and the other wanting to drown my body in the man-in-doeskin's mysterious and dark embrace. My body whirled about in confusion like a gust of devil-wind, locking my knees, sending my feet twisting into a gravel gully near the mesa's edge, hurdling me headfirst down the steep incline, bouncing and battering between the granite and burro bush until I came to a precarious and broken rest at the dusty elbow of a trail switchback.*

CHRIS MORAN

*My mouth grew hot and dry. A tingling numbness grew from where my toes started and gradually worked its way up through my shins to my thighs. My vision was commanded by a brightly swirling spiral of silver light. My heart pounded in my chest like a drunken hammer.* This is dying, I *thought. A large warm hand cradled the back of my head, another at the small of my back. I couldn't tell whether I was being lifted, or if I was falling. It wouldn't have mattered to me either way. . . .*

FLOATING IN A SEA OF OIL, twisting slowly, fluidly in a thick current of black, side to side, gently tumbling, end over end . . . a muffled roar, waves upon waves, upon waves . . . sensing . . . my arms . . . my leg . . . my hands . . . my fee . . . my stomach . . . my chest . . . my neck . . . floating, twisting, tumbling . . . separately . . . disjointed in the current . . . over and over . . . the roaring waves breaking louder . . . upon a shore . . . a cloudy, luminous shore . . . luminous yellow sand . . . pulling in my hands . . . my feet . . . my limbs . . . my torso . . . my body . . . joining . . . back together . . . slowly . . . painfully . . . coming to rest . . . resting on the shore . . . the luminous shore . . . the luminous yellow sand. . . .

*"Temple Doolin" . . . a voice . . . an echo . . . "Temple Doolin". . . . an echo reflecting off the walls of a canyon . . . "Temple Doolin" . . . a voice . . . a deep, measured baritone voice . . . the man-in-doeskin . . . "I am taking you with me" . . . Jonathan's voice . . . "I am taking you with me" . . .*

*A sensation on my face . . . on my cheek . . . breath . . . warm breath . . . "Temple Doolin, this life you have known is now past" . . . his voice . . . Jonathan's . . . close . . . full . . . deep . . .*

*"I am taking you with me, Temple Doolin, to the birthplace of the Old Keepers, older than the Chiracahua, older than the Mescalero, older than the Mogollon, and forever hence you will*

*be among them. A place which is no place, yet it will be every place you go. A place where death and life suspend between the axis of earth and heaven, and there is only the Becoming, the ever-present. A place where the dark of night shall be overcome by the light of the stars, and the stars will shine darkly—It is your only hope, dear one, as it was mine—It is a place where you may thrive and your soul may breathe for the first time. A place of great power and beauty . . .*

*"In the Becoming you will see the world as it truly is. You will see how the Gift of the Becoming must be used to stay the balance of this world, the very Earth itself, despite the bottomless greed of men's souls. You will understand the predators as you now understand the hunted, that which is excess and that which is starvation, the terrible and the pure, and you will be charged with the weight of balancing those scales wherever you find them . . .*

*"Yet for now, you must find the balance of your own life, your destiny, the purpose of your birth in this body, your man-self, your woman-self— your own place of struggle and pain and choice, where only you may choose who you will become and what shape your life . . . your lives . . . will take . . ."*

*My ears slowly filled with the sound of rattling shells and bones and pebbles and twigs and seeds. A chorus, layer upon layer, of rattles. I could make out different pitches, different rhythms, different tempos. I studied them, I tried to make sense of their language, I tried to comprehend their deeply encoded messages, then I just followed the swishing, tumbling currents of sounds like falling water, like waves of rain, like snow flurries, like eddies of cool, spiraling air . . .*

*Suddenly, I was enveloped by a dense fog of sharp sagebrush smoke. My lungs seized, I panicked and gasped for air, my body convulsed and flailed. A large, warm hand came to rest upon my chest, gently laying me supine. The weight of the hand forced me to breathe, deeply, and again, deeply. My arms grew heavy again. My legs went numb.*

*I pressed my eyes open. Jonathan's face was poised a few inches above mine, watching me intently, warmly, almost smiling. I fixed upon his eyes . . . burning a clear blue flame into mine.*

*And with strange impassivity, I watched as Jonathan bent over my torso and placed his mouth over the top of my left breast. I heard a great sucking sound like a large horse-trough draining. My muscles contracted violently at the immediate change in the rhythm of my heart. The familiar, monotonous dash-dot-dot, dash-dot-dot heartbeat that had accompanied my dull, thoughtless nineteen years of precious life stopped in a simple instant. Just stopped. My stomach sunk into a dark well. The blood in my veins thickened, slowed and came to a halt. My sense of touch, my nerves seemed to glaze over with a thick insulation of warm fluid. Yet, I managed to see, and hear, and feel, distantly, as if I were witnessing these strange events from outside of myself.*

*Jonathan's large, warm hand steadied my startled response as if he had expected it. His free hand slipped behind my head, lifting my stunned body into a puppet-like sitting position, arms hanging uselessly at my side. His head rose with me and placing his lips at the crown of my skull, blew his breath so intensely that I felt a dark, freezing wind permeate every pore of my body. I shuddered uncontrollably. A new rhythm entered my chest, a rhythm like a deep, hollow, bass drum, slow, measured—one, then another, then another, each spaced five seconds apart. I marvelled at my heartbeat's new depth, it's calm, it's peace.*

*Jonathan guided my head and body back to rest, and I closed my eyes to see a bright golden core of light, radiating a million*

*shades of shimmering color in long flowing waves, lulling me
to sleep . . . safe asleep . . .*

*MY BODY RECOVERED QUICKLY, very quickly, from my bone-
breaking fall down the mesa's jagged slope. Wounds which
would have taken weeks, if not months to repair, started healing
in a matter of hours. Three days after Jonathan brought me
through the ritual of the Becoming, the bruises, sprains, cuts
and breaks, which under "normal" circumstances would have
killed me or left me crippled for life, were all but undetectable.*

*Breaking camp, Jonathan scattered the smooth black river
stones which made up his dreaming spiral and rode his
Appaloosa mare over the surface of the yellow clay floor, reducing
its perfection to uneven piles of dust. The fire pit was buried and
the meat-smoking cribs broken and tossed into the brush. Not a
discernible sign remained that a human—that any being with
a waking consciousness—had inhabited this outcropping in
several generations. No one would ever suspect the mystery and
drama which had taken place in this simple, dark ravine.*

*We rode down though Glenwood to where Silver Creek joined
Rio de San Francisco. At the river crossing, the ferryman told
us how the Mescaleros raided Mogollon a few days earlier. In
the mayhem and bloodshed, U.S. Army Sergeant James Cooney,
the dubious hero, and money-mongering founder of that
illustrious mining town, was killed in a strange, explosive fire,
trapped in the livery stable. No other details were known. None
were needed.*

*Even now, I could not describe to you the terrible clarity, the
awful beauty in which I looked through different eyes at the
pinon pine, the yucca, the mountain jay, the gray squirrel, and
the broad expanse of sky which seemed to fall off the end of the
world. If I spoke a dozen words to the man-in-doeskin on any*

## CHRIS MORAN

*given day since our fated hunting trip, I spoke one. I was all but mute with the wonderment, grief and joy of my new being, of my own personal becoming—forever, seemingly forever, nineteen years old, a young nineteen at that, for a man. For a woman, I would be just about right. And it is not without the blackest sense of humor that I remember feeling a profound disappointment that crossing into the mysteries of the Old Keepers and crossing the barriers of human mortality did not also include crossing the physical barriers of my own sex. But, I was young . . . very young. My personal becoming, however inevitable, would be a longer, more difficult journey than my youthful mind could then imagine . . .*

*We rode west, then due north. Jonathan guided us that spring to Canon de Chelly and Canon del Muerte, centuries long sanctuaries to the Old Keepers. There we camped among the Navaho, the Dineh, who, welcomed us at a cautious, but cordial distance. While the various clan elders were familiar with our ways, they were all too aware of their people's fear of "witches" to invite us very close to their daily lives. The following spring we moved west to Hopi, and the next, on past Flagstaff to California.*

*Almost a thousand miles and over a hundred camps separated us from Mogollon. Near Havasu, a few hours from a small Chemehueva village, Jonathan remarked, almost casually, that he had exhausted his teachings in the ancient ways of the Gift of the Becoming. I watched with some puzzlement as he removed the black leather medicine-pouch around his neck and tied it to the saddle horn of his Appaloosa. It was given to him as an honor of peerage and brotherhood by a Mescalero healer shortly before we left Apache territory and started west. I guess I had grown comfortable with Jonathan's ways despite the fantastic journey which we had shared the past three years, despite the frightening and awesome teachings, despite the fact that we were in love. I guess I must have grown too comfortable. Jonathan always warned of a Receiver of the Gift growing too comfortable, or too dependent, or in any way unconscious of the world around them. I guess I had fallen prey to all three of those traps. I did not question Jonathan's gesture that evening. I did not question the dangling medicine-pouch tied to the saddle, the same pouch which he had not parted with for a single moment in three years. I did not question his brooding silence, his detachment, his terrible aura of absolute aloneness.*

*I, of course, was oblivious to the message which he attempted to telegraph to me. I was too busy playing the "ever-dutiful housewife," lost in the middle of cooking supper and fixing our bedding. Everything seemed to have a place in the world and everything was in it's place. I was too busy basking the contentment of belonging, the harmony of feeling loved, the pride of being valued. Too busy exploring the old confines of my soul beginning to stretch—birthing into a new, emerging being, beyond even the confines of my sex . . .*

*Yet, there in front of me, for the first time since I had known Jonathan, I saw a physically tired, worn, almost haggard man, as if the infinite flow of thoughts which continuously ran through his active and vital being, had finally taken their toll and drained him of his essential force. For an Old Keeper this state was a nearly impossible condition. I tried to rationalize why he would be so distracted. I tried to excuse his behavior and forgive him for what merely human part of him still occupied his being. I tried not to see the inevitable. I tried not to see that his purpose with me, his transmission of a fluid stream of magical teachings, had reached an end, and that simple love and affection could not limit his destiny to a single person, a single life . . .*

*The next morning, before the sun broke over Crossman Peak, I awakened slowly with the sense that I had been sleeping alone. I listened for the familiar and reassuring sound of Jonathan's breathing. I heard none. Quickly, I rolled over to see an empty, rumpled bearskin. Jonathan's Appaloosa was still tethered to* the palo verde, *his medicine-pouch still dangling from the saddle horn. My roan mare was gone. I drew my breath in sharply and leaped up, naked, twirling around, squinting to see if I could make out his large frame in the dull early light. Panicked, I searched the camp floor for scuff marks, or horse's hoofprints which would give me a clue to his leaving. His clothes and saddlebags were gone, yet the dust and dew on the camp floor were fresh and undisturbed. I searched the horizons back and forth, searching for any trace of movement, any glimpse of a man on horseback, any shadow, any glint of light that would tell me where I should follow, how I should pursue. . . .*

*The skyline revealed nothing, nothing but empty, motionless space. Everything was silent and calm in the blue morning light. Even the wind and the birds were still. And I knew, as I sunk back onto the damp bearskin, that I was alone . . . I knew, as I drew my knees up to my chest, that this "alone" would be my alone for a long, long time . . . I knew, as I stared into the blank air, that I would have to live my life, my lives, alone, untrusting and wary, shrouded in secrecy, and that, alone, I would endure the many, many tests of my own becoming . . .*

*I knew that this alone . . . would be alone for . . . ever . . .*

## VII.

*. . . Spiraling blue light . . . sharp flashes of red . . .*
Damned lights! They're here already! What a *scene.* I'm so

149

fucking *tired* of this shit. I'm so intensely *tired!* But this shit's *over*, baby, it's over. I'm just going to answer the door. Just *open* the motherfucker up and watch as their poor *little*, fucking brains overload on high. Fucking hysterical drag queen vampire leaping all over their sorry asses! Just *sucking* their sorry, fucking hearts out! I'll put up a good fight and then I'll just lay back and let *them* finish it. All their training in the police academy, all their training in medical school, all their training in forensics . . . shot . . . not even worth a shit in the woods!

No, I really never did have a *shred* of common sense after all!

Maybe one of them will flip out—you know, *totally* loose his nut. Maybe just one of them will . . . *know*, really know what they're up against. Maybe just one of them will know *how* to do it, really *do it* . . . They'll just say that I attacked them . . . they'll report that it was either them or me—you know, instant vampire justice . . . like all those sick, stupid movies, but *this* time, one of them will *know*, and they will be successful, they will *know* to cut and separate my neck between the third and fourth vertebrae, they will *know* to pack the uncannily bloodless wound with gunpowder and they will *know* how to fix the fuse. It will be messy, but it will be final. And they will be heroes, and *they* will be condemned to *their* lives of puking tabloid headlines and insulting, inane talk shows!

. . . And I, *I* will be released . . . liberated from ages to come of disbelieving doctors and stunned nurses; of cheap, selfish upwardly mobile ghosts driving Italian sports cars who pretend to be alive. I will be forever excused of playing balance-the-scales with the *true* homicidal bloodsuckers of this world: The lumber lords, the strip-mining and oil bosses, the investment speculators, the chemical engineers, the pharmaceutical executives—*never* again to see their shocked, pale faces as the last ounces of their sick, greedy lives are consumed before their eyes like so many ounces of Pepsi! I will no more have to endure living my lives in multiple states of perpetual sexual limbo, bouncing between the radiant truths of my soul, the incandescent desires of my heart, and the strange, slimy clay of my flesh . . .

And I will be *freed* at last from the grief of loosing another true and real love, of planting the fragile essence of my innermost being into the deepest bed of another's soul for nurturance and warmth and absolute union, only to have that vital trust crumble and dissolve—in a matter of *seconds*—into a dark, yawning well of vast and cold oblivion. Freed, *freed* of wanting, wanting more, and more . . . always more . . .

Two-Spirit. *Two*-Spirit . . . IIa! *Three*-Spirit . . . *Four*-Spirit . . . I've lost count.

And all I have to do, now, is wait for the knock at the door and calmly rise and walk across the room, straighten my clothes, smooth my hair behind my right ear, and open that door, and it will only be a moment or two before . . . I will be gone . . . but *this* time I will be *gone . . . done . . . good-bye . . . for . . . ever . . .*

EPILOGUE:

PATROLMAN EPSILON RADIOED back that a coroner was needed immediately. He excused the paramedics as they stood poised with their gurney and portable cardiac unit in the doorway of room 12A. No need here, the patrolman assessed, to waste resources. Paramedics were in short supply in this part of Los Angeles. There was no need of pronouncing death upon a body that appeared to be dead for weeks, or even months. The coroner would see to that job easily. Yet the disturbing part of this equation was that a near hysterical 911 call had been received a scant fifteen minutes earlier. The emergency reported was of a recent death, a very recent death. Resuscitation may have been possible, according to the sobbing caller. But the body on the floor appeared as withered and dry as a bundle of willow tinder. It could have been years old and, as the patrolman observed, it seemed to age by the second. There were no traces of recent activity in the room, save for an ancient, battered Packard-Bell tape recorder whirring a tail-end of spooled tape, around and around in futile, lopsided circles. Nothing else. No clothes, no newspapers, no food crumbs, no cigarette ashes. The room appeared absolutely spotless, not even a trace of dust, as if swept clean by a harsh, dry wind. The hair bristled on the back of Patrolman Epsilon's neck. He radioed for Homicide-Special Investigations.

The Detective Captain-in-charge demanded complete privacy in the drab hotel room, save for his partner, a dog-ragged lieutenant desperately pushing his pension years. He walked over to the tape recorder, switched it off, and carefully placed the tape spool in a plastic evidence bag. The uniforms and the coroners were ordered to vacate the scene immediately upon Special Investigations' arrival.

One corner to corner view of the spotless room and Captain Bogan knew that all that would bear fruit in this case was the condition of the body and possibly the spool of tape in his pocket. Knowing instinctively that a search for prints, or hair, or disposables would be useless, he knelt near the twisted corpse and staightened its spine so that the collapsing face raised toward the ceiling. He opened the corpse's shirt where his eyes settled on a large, fresh puckering wound just above the body's left nipple. Then he watched with certain expectation as the wound swiftly dried and closed in upon itself. He closed the corpse's shirt and stood up.

"Get Epsilon in here, George. Tell him to supervise this Doe's removal to the cooler. We have nothing here, nothing anymore."

"Sure, John," the lieutenant replied.

The Captain-in-charge walked back across the room, his right hand thrust inside of his jacket pocket, gripping the spool of tape until his knuckles ached. He stood at the window staring intently down at the flashing red and blue lights of the patrolmen's squad cars. Then, slowly raising the creaking hotel window, the Captain lifted himself onto the fire escape and stood erect to carefully scan the city's jagged horizon. The Santa Ana winds gusseted the trouser legs around his worn hide boot shafts and tousled his thick, black mane of hair.

The sun was half an hour away from rising upon another day in the old, downtown garment district. A deep bluish-green cast draped over the dingy brick and stucco buildings which lined 7th Street.

Det. Capt. John Bogan slowly searched the skyline, searching for a brief telltale waver of light, searching for the dim shimmer of a fluttering shadow, piercing the smokey, dull pre-dawn. . . . searching. . . . searching. His eyes burned a clear blue flame.

# A Poor Imitation

## DAVID N. WILSON

*She wanted
a better life —
he gave her
a better
death!*

 WRITE THIS KNOWING it will appear as fiction. It amuses me. Years passed in the lonely solitude of shadows multiply the need for amusement.

I have seen things undreamed, lived as a nightmare breath of wind on nights uncounted, run with the wild wolves 'neath glowing moons and viewed them crimson through predatory eyes. I have dined with poets who are now ash and whitened bone, have courted beauty barely remembered to the world through the poor reflection of words—as if viewed through the cracked and broken glass of time-warped windows. I have shared the blood of kings. The tales I could tell—and perhaps, in time, will tell—are myriad and dark. For now, a recent meeting between myself and one mortal woman fills my mind. I am given to deep thought. Nothing else, save hunger, presses me.

I walked at midnight among the refuse-strewn streets of what passes for civilization in this age. I am not certain that this description pleases me, but I will let it stand. The moon shone, three-quarters full, and bright as silvered sunlight. I was well-fed, content to walk and to think. Such a calm, emotionless moment is a rarity to me, and I savored it like well aged wine. Then I found the girl.

The alley was deserted, or seemed so, and I nearly passed it without a glance. A silver glimmer, brighter than that of moonlight alone, winked from the shadows. Curious, I entered the darkened, cave-like orifice. Garbage flowed over the sides of a rusted garbage bin; bottles and cans littered the oil-stained pavement. My eyes traced shadowed shapes, picking my goal from the deeper ebon, where she cowered beneath the pages of a discarded newspaper.

Her eyes were dull; little of the light of life shone from them, and I was puzzled. My senses, predatory and exact, pick details when most would see a blur. I knew she was young . . . perhaps fifteen. Her heartbeat had gained a bit in strength at my approach, but only partially in fear. There was something else in her gaze, in the quivering nervous twitching of her skin, something that drew me.

I reached down gently and parted the papers, pulling them firmly from her grasping hands. I searched her eyes more carefully, searched for an answer in her soul.

"What you want, mister?" she blurted, shifting fear to false bravado in the way of the streets. I nearly smiled. I did not answer. I had yet to pinpoint the itching at my senses that her gaze brought. She squirmed under my scrutiny, her fear returning.

"Hey, you wanna party, mister?" she asked, a pleading, yellowish taint filtering through the white-fear surface of her eyes. It was then that I saw it, and I was stunned. The hunger, it bled from her like sweat from a running horse, like the pus from an infected wound. I recognized the hunger. I share it. And yet there was something wrong.

"You do not appear dressed for a party," I observed, my curiosity thoroughly aroused. I have seen my hunger mirrored in other eyes—can still recall the hunger that drank my own mortality, emptying that part of me I can never truly fill. She hungered, this small, pathetic girl, and yet she lived.

"You know what I mean," she said sullenly, casting her eyes to the ground, then sweeping them upward to take in my form, ending in the depths of my own. She was caught as surely as any rat in a trap. I looked away. The pulsing of her blood called out to me, begged me to drink. I was not ready—not until I understood.

"I assume you wish my body?" I asked, watching her reaction carefully.

"No, I mean, yeah . . . but don't you 'wish' mine? I mean, I'm broke, mister, and I'm hungry. You ain't a bad lookin' dude, and I *really* need some money."

"I see your hunger," I answered, holding out my hand to help her rise. "But tell me, for I see that food is not your concern, what it is that you hunger for?"

"What kind of weird shit is this?" she demanded, trying to free her hand. I held on. "I mean, are you some kind of weird cop, or a pervert, or what?"

"I am neither," I answered, pulling her nearer and calming her with a short sip from my eyes. I saw her mouth gape, then grow slack. I looked away again, but now my own hunger rose, unbidden.

"Tell, me," I commanded, "tell me what it is you seek. Quickly."

"I . . . I need a fix, okay mister? I need it bad. Leon, he'll hook me up if I come up with the cash. I just want to hit up—have to. You interested? I . . . I kinda like you, the clothes and all. You seem so—clean."

I nearly laughed aloud, something long passed from my "life."

"You know nothing of me," I told her. "You are telling me

that a drug has done this to you? You need this drug more than food—or sleep? Why?"

"I need to be high," she nearly whined. "It makes me stronger—smarter. I make more money when I'm high. I get sick when I'm straight for too long. My skin crawls. I can't stand it then . . . I have to hit up."

I turned once more and gazed into eyes that were a man-made, cheap imitation of the curse on my soul. I felt her weakness, took from her her hunger, and replaced it with my eyes, only my eyes. She moved close against me, and I folded her into my arms, lost in my own need. Memories, as always, filled me as her blood became mine. Her memories.

I saw the needles, the powder. I knew her fear, her shame.

I lived her pain and she learned of mine. I saw the yellow sheen of poison drift from her eyes, followed by the pale, lifeless lustre of undead light. Her lips curved into a blissful smile of release.

I supported her for a moment, my mind lost on roadways far away. Lifting her limp form in my arms, I strode back through the empty streets, returning to my own place of rest, her weight no more than a feather to my blood-strengthened arms. I placed her gently in a crate beside my own, cushioned on mounds of richest earth. Covering her, I slept.

For two nights I stood vigil, departing only when the need to feast grew unbearable, dragging at my flesh like a barbed collar and chain. At midnight on the third day, her eyes fluttered, then opened, and she arose, regarding me with quiet awe. Hunger flickered wildly in the newly cleansed depths of her eyes.

"What have I become?" she asked. "What the *hell* did you do?"

"You should know . . ." I answered, "You should have seen

it in my eyes. I 'hit up.' "

Seeming to contemplate my words, she suddenly spoke again. "I'm hungry. It hurts . . . what do I do?"

"Feed," I said simply.

I watched her melt into the night and I lost myself yet again to contemplation. So many years my curse has haunted my soul; so many hearts have paid the price of my continuance. In all of those years, man has striven, in his own suicidal way, to recreate my curse. As always, when mirroring powers beyond his ken, man has failed. My hunger is pure, my power constant. His drugs ruin him, even as he hungers.

She is more alive now than before, I think. That is an irony worthy even of my own centuries-honed sense of humor. I am the drug that has set her free. She wanted hunger, it is hers. May eternity teach its lessons. I must feed, then sleep. I am not a mystery . . . I am a truth. It is man, as always, that is the mystery.

# The Croquet Mallet Murders

## KEVIN ANDREW MURPHY

*It was a most
unusual world . . .
and he was a
most unusual
detective.*

T WAS FRIDAY, and I was running late. Some genius once said the dead travel quickly, but no one travels quickly in LA, and anyway, I'm not dead—I'm cursed. Big difference.

Not that there's anything wrong with being dead, mind you—some of my best friends are ghosts and zombies—but a vampire (or sangroid as we prefer to be called) isn't dead. Cursed, yeah. Allergic to sunlight? Fer sure. But dead? Hell no. At least not by the laws of the Island of California, or the pronouncements of Queen Calafia and Emperor Norton, and those were what mattered.

When you're a vampire, the worst damned thing about Los Angeles is the Ventura Freeway, or should I say the fucking El Camino Real. Father Serra and the rest of his merry monks warded the whole thing so that folk like me—ie. guys who the damn fucking wonderful Holy Mother Church decided were 'evil'—couldn't set foot on it until after midnight. Or fly over it, for that matter, unless you wanted to risk passing out. It's a fucking public nuisance, and I don't like my tax dollars going towards it, whether or not it's some damn historical landmark from the days when Father Serra and his Franciscan bastards ran around the island terrorizing the natives and staking people like me.

But I'm getting off the subject. I was running late, and I didn't have time to ask a griffin to fly me across the Ventura, or to wait for the Witching Hour to start, so I just got up to cruising velocity and slammed right across. Kinda dangerous, I'll admit, but it did the trick. Pop-in, pop-out.

By the way, I don't turn into a bat, if that's what you're wondering. One of the few perks of my strain of the curse is that I can fly, and in my own body too. No bats or wolves for this bloodsucker. And since that body weighs in at three-hundred plus, I can get a lot of force behind it. No trouble crossing the Ventura—used to be nose-tackle for USC. Of course, that's also why that bastard Martin put the bite on me, not that it did him much good. (I'm glad they staked him too. No one should have to live with this shit, and the only thing worse than being a vampire is being a servitor vampire. You have no idea how humiliating it is to have to grovel at the feet of the asshole who killed you and go "Yassa massa!" to everything he says.)

But anyway, I got to the roof of the Nikon Tower, turned into mist, and slipped on down the vent to The Outcast Club. That's where I work. Big, fancy bar, small restaurant and dance floor, large balcony and live music on weekends. If you know the LA scene, you know the type of place I'm talking about.

I'm the night bouncer, as I bet you could guess. No one messes with a guy my size, especially if he's got vampiric strength, not that there aren't people who might try it at the Outcast Club. We get all types, so long as they're cursed and not welcome at the other clubs: vampires, werewolves, fox spirits, phantoms. All types, and that means all types of trouble. And what I can't handle with sheer brute strength, I can usually manage by just by taking off my shades and letting 'em look into the ol' steely blues. The vampiric fascination does the rest.

Don't usually like doing that—I remember how creepy it was getting hypnotized the first time I locked eyes with a vampire—but then again, it's better than dealing with a werewolf who's tied on one too many. That's the reason most of us vamps wear shades, by the way. It's not that the light's are too bright; it's just that "Yes, Master" gets really boring after the third time you hear it. Or at least it should, unless you're some kind of sicko.

The only guy tougher than me at the bar is my best bud and fellow bouncer, Carlos. He isn't really much to look at— tall, skinny, pretty-boy type, and most of that handsomeness is Glamour anyway. If you got a look at him in the mirror, you'd see he's going bald and has hair growing about everywhere else. But he isn't a werewolf, if that's what you're thinking. Nah, Carl's something a lot tougher—one of the Jaetatura, which means he has the Evil Eye. Only a pair of spellproof wraparounds keeps you safe from the power in his eyes, and if he takes the shades off—woah boy! Pure, unadulterated bad luck, and that packed more of a punch or a threat than I ever could. Last thing the damned wanted to deal with was another curse.

Carl was over by the mirror, this big Turn-of-the-Century affair in a carved-oak frame. The Club keeps it around 'cause it's a gate to the astral and makes it a lot easier for the ghosts and phantoms to come inside. I'd been told it had once belonged to Cecil B. De Mille, and legend had it that if you looked into it too long, you'd see your doom.

Not that that was much of an issue for me, since I couldn't

see my reflection anyway. Carl, however, was looking his doom right in the face, his doom being Charlie, his fetch. Carl's doubly cursed, 'cause besides having the Evil Eye, he knows that one day Charlie's going to step out of the mirror and come for him.

Makes for a weird life, Carl says, but Charlie—aside from being a damned fetch—is occasionally useful, and doesn't mind helping Carl out on rare occasions, so long as it fits with whatever agenda fetches follow. Don't ask me exactly what a fetch is supposed to do—that's a question for a necromancer, and I'm just an ordinary vamp—but it has something to do with Charlie knowing the day Carl is going to die, and Charlie teases him about it all the time, without ever telling him when it is.

A vamp's ears are really sharp too, and once I'd resumed solid form, I could hear exactly what Carl was saying: "Psst, Charlie." Carl snuck a look at his reflection, which, as I said, looked nowhere near as good as he did in real life.

Charlie, I think, could follow Carl's thoughts, or at least mine: "Well at least you get to *look* like Mr. Handsome. I have to look like this all the time."

"Keep it down, Charlie," Carlos hissed.

"Why? So people won't talk?" Charlie took off his wrap-arounds and polished them with a bar cloth. The fetch did tricks like that all the time, and I'm not sure if seeing Charlie's eyes was giving Carl and me a whammy right then and there. "What can I do you for, partner?" Charlie put the glasses back on and smiled.

Carlos leaned close to his reflection, almost nose to nose with Charlie. "Is Jack over there?"

"Jack's a vampire, doofus," Charlie whispered back. "No reflection, no fetch. His fetch died the day he joined the undead."

"I meant is he dead."

I know Charlie saw me, but he didn't let on. Like I said, he liked giving Carl nasty surprises. "Nope," I said, putting my hands on Carl's shoulders.

Carl whirled, twisting out of my grip.

Hard to be as fast as a vampire, though. "Hiya, Carl." I pinned him to the mirror and grinned. "Talking to yourself?"

"Only in a manner of speaking."

I looked past him into the De Mille mirror. "Hiya, Charlie."

The fetch didn't respond, pretending he was just an ordinary reflection. Standard tricks for Charlie.

Carlos pulled me away from the mirror. "You're late."

I smiled, feeling my fangs slide out. "Hey, Carl, vampires are always late."

"That joke's been around longer than you've been dead, Jack. I'm serious."

"Hey, don't get all bent out of shape. You'll get the overtime." I punched him in the shoulder, lightly. "And I'm not dead— I'm cursed, no matter what your Pope says. And pardon me, but I'm starving." I pushed him aside and reached into the bar's refrigerator, pulling out a pint flask. "I hate drinking this stuff cold. . . ."

Carl, as I said, was my best bud, and knew what I needed. He reached into his jacket and took out an identical bottle, warmed by the heat of his body. "Don't drink that junk. Here." He held out the flask.

I put down the cold one and took the bottle from Carl. "Thanks." I bit off the neck, not minding where the glass cut my lips, and tossed it back.

You have no idea how good blood tastes when it's warm— it's the greatest stuff in the world, at least if you're a vampire. Of course, this was only alchemical sanquine, but it tasted just about as good, especially when you get as hungry as I do.

I drained the last of it and threw it in the wastebasket, mopping my face with a bar towel and spitting out the last few bits of glass. That always freaked Carl out, but he still picked up the bottle of cold sanquine and put it in his inner pocket. "I'll get this warmed up for you too."

"Thanks." Like I said, Carl was my best bud. Not many breathing folk who'd do that for a vampire, let alone Catholics who'd do it.

Carl, however, looked kind of upset, and there was that whole weird business with him talking to Charlie. He only brought Charlie into it if something was really eating him, not that he could keep anything from the fetch as it was.

I brushed my hair back and grinned, teeth back in line. "What's the problem? Am I messing up some hot date?"

He looked real serious, so I don't think that was it. "No," Carl said simply, "I was worried, that's all." He reached under the bar and pulled out the evening edition of *The Trib.* "The nutcase with the croquet mallet struck three more times."

What blood I had in me suddenly went cold. "Fu . . ." I took off my shades and unfolded the paper.

"That's just that the police know about," Carl said. "Those are just the *registered* vampires."

I looked at him. "We prefer the term *sangroids*, Catholic."

"Ease off, Jack, and put you shades back on." Carl picked them up and stuck them back on my face. His own shades had the added perk of keeping my Fascination out, the same as they kept his Evil Eye in, so I wasn't suddenly having to deal with him gaping like a dead fish and saying, "Master . . ."

His next line was about as far from that as you could get: "I don't know why you wear mirrorshades anyway. They don't reflect the bridge of your nose and it looks really silly. Anyway, if I was going for the whole Catholic bit, I'd be reciting 'Hail Mary's' at you right now."

I winced as he said the name.

"Sorry," Carl said quickly.

"Watch it with those names of power."

"I said I was sorry, Jack. You're my housemate for Chri— For someone-who's-name-I-shouldn't-take-in-vain-especially-around-vampires' sake," Carlos quickly corrected himself. "Or 'sangroids' sake' if you want that."

I shoved the paper at him. "Have you read this?"

"Hell yeah," Carlos said. "Why do you think I was so worried?"

"But just listen to this:" I folded the paper. " 'Three more known vampires were found staked this afternoon, the latest in a series of impalings centering in the Los Angeles basin. The bodies were found beheaded—' " I gritted my fangs. "Why doesn't it say, 'Three more Los Angeles County residents were found brutally murdered and mutilated'? Huh, why not? Why's it so damn important to mention they're vampires so it'll seem okay? So people can say, 'Oh, it was just a vampire, no need to fear for *our* lives or do anything about it.' Huh, why?"

"Because there ain't no justice and the press is almost as biased as the police, that's why." Carlos looked away, staring at the wall. "You think I don't know that, Jack? I'm cursed too, remember, and people like Jaetatura even less than they like vampires. And there's less of us than there are of you."

"Trade you," I said. "Trade you right now."

"And I'd trade both of you, except it's impossible." We both looked: It was Jim, the werewolf lawyer. Jim was this fancy, uptown guy, but played it cool and didn't hide what he was. He was always decked out to the nines too, silvered hair slicked back to show off his widow's peak, and wolf-grey

Italian suits set off with gold—never silver—cuff links and tie tacks. You had to give it to him; the man had class.

"You'd be out of a job, Jim," I said. "You couldn't swear on the B— on that Christian book."

"Then I'd take the Mahabharata." Jim grinned, wolfish. "Equality of Religious Oaths Act, 1926." He tossed his briefcase on an empty table. "So who's on duty anyway?"

Carl thumbed to me.

"Better stand by the door and look imposing then." Jim raised a clawed finger, leaning over slightly. "Sylvia! Bloody Mary please."

I set the paper on top of his briefcase and pointed to the article. "Read this."

Jim scanned it. "Fun case for the D.A.'s office if they ever catch the bastard," he concluded.

"Is that all you can say?" You have no idea how pissed I was. Some nutcase was running around turning my people into lawn ornaments and all he could say was "fun case."

"Simmer down, Jack. You can have some of my tranquilizer philtre." The werewolf pushed the newspaper aside with one hairy pentacle-palmed hand, then took the Bloody Mary as the waitress came by. "Thanks, Sylvia." He took a sip. "Jack, all I meant was that it will be a hard case to prosecute if they even catch the person responsible."

"Hard case? It's coldblooded, premeditated *murder*." I leaned forward, squeezing the back of one of the chairs to keep from throttling him.

Jim twiddled his celery stalk. "By the laws of the Island of California. Not by the laws of Mexico, or the Catholic church, which recently has been getting more powerful." He sucked the tomato juice off the celery stalk, then crunched it contemplatively.

"I don't give a shit about Mexico or the damn church!" The chair made splintering noises under my fingers. "It's *murder*."

"I'm not disputing that. However, the alleged murderer is probably someone who's had some family member killed by a vampire—and who's probably a devout Catholic—" He gave a pointed look to Carlos. "—and unless there's a very talented prosecution—which I doubt—they'll get off with some form of temporary insanity and be spellbound or sent to a mental hospital for a couple years. I'm not being cold, Jack, just practical, and I don't like the situation any more than you do."

The chair disintegrated under my hands. "Fuck that! If I go temporarily insane from hunger and kill someone, I get put to *death*. Same thing with you, Jim. And if someone's trying to murder me and I kill them, I still get put to death!"

Jim raised a claw. "Only if they're killed vampirically or lycanthropically. The law is very explicit. If someone with a Van Helsing complex comes after you, and you, say, blow them away with a wand, that's self defense and you're home free."

"How many times has that happened?"

The lawyer reflected. "Three," he said finally. "Two acquitted, one unstaked after appeal after execution, the Seabright Case, which is what defined the law in the first place."

"Oh that's fucking lovely," I said. "Just what we need. Fangs are illegal and wands aren't. You can assault people with deadly weapons so long as they aren't your own body."

"Jack, we both know why the laws were passed."

I glared at the werewolf. "Yeah, I guess we do. Doesn't that make us all so fucking happy."

"Better than Mexico, my friend."

I took up my position by the door, picking the splinters out my hands with my fangs. They hurt the way only miniature wooden stakes could. "Only in some ways, Jim. Only in some ways."

IT WAS A COUPLE HOURS LATER before I finally cooled down. It had been a pretty bad scene. Carl had left without giving me my *sanguine*. and Jim had followed pretty soon after. I was feeling like a first-class heel. I mean, Carl meant well, and was worried about me and everything, and I couldn't blame him for not being a vampire. And I really couldn't blame Jim for being so flip about the whole thing either. He was dosed up on wolfsbane and valerian root to keep him from getting upset about anything, 'cause while it might be bad enough when I rolled my terrible eyes and gnashed my terrible teeth, what I could do as a vamp weren't nothing compared to the bad scene that would go down if Jim got all hot under the collar. Werewolves who couldn't keep their tempers tended to get sniped with silver wands, and that was the last thing I'd wish on Jim.

I just stood by the door, looming, and doing a pretty good job of being a bouncer. No one wanted to mess with me. Least not that night.

Then things changed.

Like an apparition, she arrived at the stroke of midnight, but through the door, not the mirror.

She was alive. I could feel it, in my crotch and in my teeth. Damn, how I could feel it. My fangs were just about jabbing me in the chin, and my dick had gotten tangled in my boxers. I wanted to shove everything back into place, but I was playing bouncer and all the eyes in the place were on me, especially hers.

Her eyes were green, like cat's-eye marbles, and she was

looking up at me from under a flip of long blond hair, the color oat straw got in the sun. Damn, how many years ago was that? It had been a long time since anything had made me remember the sunlight.

Her skin was white though, like cream next to the blood red cashmere sweater dress she wore, plunging neckline and all. And she was tall, maybe even six feet. The kind of height a man my size liked in a woman. Dressed to kill. Or bite. Or something like that. Where did a woman get off dressing that way, especially around vampires?

"This the Outcast Club?" she asked. There wasn't a trace of Spanish in her accent. A Northerner, I guessed, probably from San Francisco or Tahoe.

I willed my fangs back into line with my other teeth and nodded, glad that there were at least some parts of me I had control over. My dick was straining against my underwear, my fangs were wanting to come out too, and I tried not to look at the fine blue veins beneath her skin. But damn, there were instincts.

I looked into her eyes instead, and that helped, at least with the fangs.

"Cover charge?"

I shook my head. "Nah. No cover. Club's free to anyone who wants to be here." Damn she was beautiful.

She smiled then, and I smiled back, fangs all but receded. "Valerie," she said, extending her hand. She shifted the weight of a shoulder bag on her other arm.

I put out my hand. "Jack. Welcome to the club." Her fingers were warm and living, and even though my veins were still half dry, I felt my pulse start up.

"You're the bouncer, right?"

I grinned. "How'd you guess?"

Valerie smiled again. "Oh, I get a feeling about these things. Sixth Sense, you know." She readjusted her shoulder bag. "Could you show me the club?"

I glanced around. No trouble anywhere, and I could be at the door in a fingersnap if any trouble did come in. "Sure."

I put an arm around her shoulder and she didn't seem to mind. The warmth seeping through her sweater felt good. That was half of what I needed. Blood's nothing without the warmth of life. Sometimes, when I've just fed really well, for a minute or two I feel like I'm alive again. Alive in the regular run-around-in-the-sun sense, I mean. A vampire's still alive, but it's not often that you really feel that way. You don't just need blood from other people. You need warmth.

"Well," I said, leading her further into the club, "this is it, the Outcast Club, hangout of the cursed and bewitched but still successful of Los Angeles, if that isn't a contradiction in terms."

I glanced over to the De Mille mirror and checked Valerie out through the space where my reflection should have been. Her image was there, same as she was beside me. No illusions, no Glamour, no hint of any wereform or altershape. With her eyes and the way she walked, I'd been half expecting a werecat. But whatever her curse was, it wasn't anything the mirror could show.

Valerie paused, catching my glance, and looked past me. "The De Mille Mirror?" she said. "I've read about it."

"Most of what they say is true." I shrugged. "A few things, well, I'm not too sure."

"Like what?"

I shrugged again. "If you look into it too long, you're supposed to see your death." Valerie turned away. "Don't worry. The only person I know who's done that is Carlos, and he's always talking to his fetch anyway. Doesn't matter which mirror he looks in."

"Isn't that dangerous?"

"Nah. Charlie doesn't count as an omen till Carl sees him in *this* world. And only Charlie knows when that's going to happen, and maybe even he doesn't. Charlie won't let on."

Valerie smiled. "Your friend named his fetch?"

"His fetch named his fetch." I led her out onto the balcony. "You can't tell Charlie anything."

The night was cooler than usual for spring in Los Angeles, and there was the smell of rain in the air. Witchfire and faerie light flickered from the skyline below, catching in the windows of the financial district, while the infamous Los Angeles' faze sparkled here and there with pixie dust and other pollution.

I took my arm from around her and leaned back against the railing so I could have a clear view of the bar. "And this, of course, is the balcony. That's pretty much it for the club. Live music nine to one Friday through Sunday, well-drink specials on Tuesdays, lots of the usual club stuff—we've got a calendar—and a few arrangements for the lycanthropes and sangroids." Jack grinned. "And that's it."

"Any rules?"

"No takeoffs or landings on the balcony, even if your flight's part of yourself." I levitated a couple inches, then dropped and gave her a half-grin. "We can't have it for insurance reasons. The roof's only one floor up anyway, and there's a broomcheck and an elevator and stairwell. If you've got any of the Eyebites," I touched my sunglasses, "please wear shades. The same with any other curse or blessing you can't control. And if you've got something you can't help at all, like a Silver Tongue, it's considered good form to tell people anyway. And no Holy Words, of any religious background, please."

"Clear enough." Valerie looked up at me, eyes almost on my level. "You don't turn into a bat?"

She didn't sound afraid, just curious. I liked that. "Nah, not that sort of a vampire. Or sangroid, I should say. Next think you know I'll be saying I'm dead." I laughed. "Yeah, no bats or wolves for me. But I can do a pretty mean cloud of mist, and I can fly like nobody's business."

"And you can step on holy ground without any trouble?"

"From midnight till three, for what it's worth." I shrugged. "How'd you know?"

"Just put two and two together." She looked pensive. "*Vampyr Magus Rex*, right?"

"Yeah. You're not some sort of vampire groupie, are you?"

She shook her head. "No, far from it, just did a little research. *Magus Rex* is one of the rare ones. Powerful, too."

"Lucky me."

"Sorry," she said quickly. "It's just when something's that rare, you never think you're going to meet someone with it."

"That's what I thought too." I didn't bother to hide the bitterness. "Lucky for everyone I'm not some power-mad nutcase like the guy who got me." The night wind blew around me, sucking away my warmth. I moved forward into the lee of the building. "The *Magus Rex* variant does have some perks, but having rats swarm the financial district is not my idea of a useful ability. I hate rats."

Valerie laughed and looked back into the bar. "I notice you've got a mug rack."

"Yep, hooks for all the regulars. There's good ale, if your partial to that, or you can keep a mug here for, well, you wouldn't need that anyway, but some people stop by for coffee in the afternoons." I went back to the door. "At least that's what Carl said. Wouldn't know myself."

"I understand."

She didn't, but if there's one thing I'd learned that evening, it was that you didn't make points by being self-righteous. Everyone at the Outcast Club had fates to lament, and my curse sure wasn't the worst. Why anyone as beautiful as Valerie . . . Well, frankly, I was curious. "Let me introduce you to the regulars. One thing, though, since everyone's going to ask anyway: What's your curse?"

"We all have our crosses to bear. I prefer to keep mine hidden." Valerie put her fingers lightly on my arm and I felt a thrill of warmth and pleasure. "That okay?"

"Yeah, that's okay." I laughed and felt my fangs slide out. I let them stay; I wasn't keeping anything secret, and Valerie hadn't balked or stared once. "I'd prefer if everyone kept their crosses hidden anyway."

Valerie laughed back and shouldered her bag. "I can understand that."

"Good," I said, "let me introduce you around."

IT WASN'T HER TRUE NAME or anything, but at least I got her calling card: Valerie M—— I think the M stood for Maple or Marchinski or something like that, but it looked a lot more elegant and mysterious the way it was, and was a good enough key to get most crystal balls to work, so I didn't ask. I wasn't going to press my luck.

I'd also got her to agree to a date the next evening, 'round nine. Thursdays were my night off, and with the Croquet Mallet Murderer running around, the last thing I wanted to do was stay home organizing my socks.

Vamps have more than enough of that sort of thing as it is anyway. Being a vampire is really dull. Most normal folk— including me, before I got bit—think vampires have a great time, running around hypnotizing people by night, and sleeping in their coffins by day.

I wish.

As I guess you've figured out, hypnotizing people is really boring unless your some sort of sicko. The flying's kinda fun, I'll admit, and the strength is a bit of a kick, but then I was used to being stronger than most everyone anyway. And turning into mist is more just plain weird than useful.

But as for sleeping in a coffin all night, only weirdos or people with particularly nasty curses sleep in coffins, and I only wish I slept from sunup to sundown. Most of the day, when you're a vampire, you hang around in your basement apartment, organizing your sock drawer, getting a little sleep, and waiting for the sun to go down.

I'm luckier than most vamps 'cause in a pinch, I can call up some mist and fog and a little bit of an overcast, which lets me go out 'round dawn and dusk without the nasty ol' fireball frying my ass. But then again, I live in Venice Beach, and if you think the sun is bad, you haven't had to deal with a bunch of irate sidewalk vendors and tanning gods who think you've messed up the weather. I learned early on that it was a lot better to just stay inside and organize my socks than try to deal with that. You can't hypnotize ten people at once, and even if you hypnotize one, you have to bite 'em to make it stick, and that's illegal anyway.

I apologized to Carl for having been such a dick the night before. It was okay, though. Carl gave me the bottle of *sanguine* he'd forgotten to give me, and he and Charlie ribbed me a lot about my upcoming date.

Then Carl brought in the morning paper. The police had found another body, plus croquet stake and trademark hammer and minus head. The count was up to nine.

"Oh—Oh shit, Carl." I leaned my head forward, panting with the strain. "I want to say the name of some G— some divinity, and I can't. Do it for me."

Carl sat down at the kitchen table, looking over the paper. "Jesus Christ," he supplied. "Mary, Mother of God."

I winced as he said both of them and snarled instinctively, fangs coming out. But I felt a bit better for the shock. "Thanks, Carl. I—I needed that."

He patted me on the back. "It's okay, Jack. Listen, I'll stop by the Cathedral and light a candle for you, okay? You may not be able to pray for yourself, but I can pray for the both of us."

"And you'll need it," said Charlie from the mirror on the wall of the dinette.

"What?" Carl said. "What do you mean, Charlie?"

Charlie decided he'd do one of his favorite tricks then and pretended he was just an ordinary reflection, letting Carl press his nose up against the glass and curse up a blue streak. I winced a couple more times, but, as I said, in a perverse way it felt good.

In the end, Carl had to say his goodbyes and get off to the Cathedral and then the Club to open for the day.

I hung around until nightfall, door locked tight, then turned into mist the moment the sun went down and slipped out through the cracks.

I don't think I'd ever bothered to keep keys since I became a vampire. I guess the mist bit was okay. I'd always been losing my keys before then, and it was nice not to have to remember them.

Valerie, luckily, lived this side of the Ventura, in one of the nice high rises on the edge of Beverly Hills. Unfortunately, a card and an address didn't count as an invitation, and neither did "Pick me up around nine." I couldn't even get into the lobby to ring her bell—Not only didn't I have an invitation, but the landscaper had put in a bridge and an ornamental stream. Running water; one of the few examples in Los Angeles, and I had to run into it.

It's a pain in the butt sometimes being a vampire. Lots of normal little things you can't do that regular people take for granted.

Luckily, there were apartment numbers stenciled on the balconies for those of us who could fly, and the stream only went across the courtyard, not in a moat around the building. Of course, I still couldn't set foot on the balcony without express permission, but nothing stopped me from grabbing a handful of pebbles from the walkway, then levitating a few feet outside her apartment and pitching them at the patio door.

I was glad, too, that I'm not the type of vamp who has to count every pebble or piece of birdseed he finds on the ground before he can pass over them, otherwise that pebbled walk would have been a nightmare. I've met a couple guys with that variant of the curse, and the only thing worse than forced anal retentiveness is the *Sesame Street* jokes you have to put up with.

Me, the curse just forced to be ridiculously polite, and made me give up party crashing for the rest of my life. Of course, since I couldn't drink beer anymore, that wasn't as much of a problem. And running water, as I said, usually wasn't an issue in Los Angeles.

After about the fourth pebble, Valerie pulled aside the curtain and looked out. A moment later she opened the sliding glass door and slipped out onto the balcony. "Jack, what are you doing out here?"

I was kicking back in my imaginary lounge chair, making it look as if there were an invisible swimming pool about fifteen stories up. I waved to the ground. "Big sign down there. 'Private Property. Residents and their Invited Guests Only.' Never got a proper invitation, so I couldn't even get into the lobby. Not to mention the trouble with the pebbled path and the little stream." I grinned. "Never dated a vampire before, huh? This is about the most vamp-unfriendly building I've ever seen. And I can't set foot on your balcony until you invite me."

Valerie gave me a strange look and began to step back through the sliding glass door. "Let me get my things. I'll meet you out front."

The door slid shut and I heard the lock click as the drape fell down, hiding the apartment. I shrugged. She wasn't the first woman not to invite a guy in on the first date, and I'll admit even I was careful with my invitations with vampires. Having someone able to slip through your keyhole anytime he wanted wasn't the most reassuring thing in the world.

I drifted on down and hung out in one of the trees beside the walkway. Valerie came out a couple minutes later. She was wearing this velvet dress, midnight blue, with a really wide, low collar and her hair back in a long French braid with ribbons in it.

Like I said, that woman knew how to dress to turn a vampire on. Everything but a tattoo with arrows saying 'Bite Here,' and honestly, I'd seen those before and I thought they were kind of tacky. Valerie looked just the right type of woman for my type of vampire.

She came down the walkway, clutching the big leather carryall which she seemed to prefer to the more usual evening bag. I waited till she was just about under me before I announced my presence. "Hiya!"

She just about jumped out of her skin, or at least her dress, and she did drop her purse.

I jumped down and picked it up for her. "Sorry," I said. "I know I'm a little big to be climbing trees, but I never can resist."

She took her purse back, not looking at all amused. I shrugged and grinned. "I got to admit I'm a little nervous too. That nut with the croquet mallet is running around somewhere, and I don't feel very safe just standing out on the sidewalk."

"Nut?" Valerie asked.

"Haven't you been reading the papers?" I asked. "Some wacko with a thing against vampires is running around staking us down with croquet wickets, then whacking off the heads and leaving the mallets with the bodies."

Valerie readjusted the strap of her shoulder bag. "Oh. Yeah, some of the vampires were talking about it at the Club."

I grinned and I let my fangs show. "If you don't mind, I'd like to stick to well lit places with lots of people. I was thinking of Westwood."

She looked a little disappointed, but then smiled and put her fingers on my arm. "That'd be fine."

Valerie, as I said, lived on the edge of Beverly Hills, so there was no trouble finding a griffin, and one with a really nice chariot too. I gave Valerie a hand up and belted her in, but the griffin saw the flash of my fangs, so he didn't say anything about me just hanging out on the edge.

We took off and I picked up one of the mantles from the back of the chariot and wrapped it around her against the night chill. Her warmth felt good against me, and it was a nice, short romantic flight to Westwood.

The elves had really gone all out and the trees of Westwood were done up with faerie lights and elf fire, the shops and theatres in between filled with throngs of people. Just the sort of place I wanted to be on a night like this.

The griffin landed in one of the taxi stands and I helped

Valerie out and paid him. Valerie had some money out already. "I thought we were going Dutch."

I shrugged. "I never have to pay much for cab fare, and I don't have any food bills, so just let me treat you tonight. It's nice enough to get a chance to go out with a beautiful woman."

Valerie blushed and I felt my fangs slide out at the sight of blood. I looked away and let her take my arm, feeling her warmth as we wandered off into the crowds.

If you've been to Westwood, I probably don't need to describe it. Lots of shops with books and clothes and musical crystals and alchemists with potions and so on. We stopped by one of those, *Lily Hernandez*. Lily specializes in designer *sanquine* and I have to say that her stuff tastes a lot better than government rations, and Lily's keeps it ready and warmed in a sand bath. Expensive as hell, fer sure, but it's great stuff, and I'd saved up enough that I could afford to splurge on a bottle and a bag of sand to keep it warm.

I paid and turned to Valerie. "Where do you want to go for dinner?"

"I—" She paused. "I'm sort of new to the area. I don't know many places. Nowhere too fancy."

"Howbout the Hamburger Hamlet? I liked that when-Well, when I still ate solid food."

Valerie had a strange expression, but then shrugged and put her hand on my arm. "That sounds nice."

The Hamlet is a great place, and's about as fancy as you can make a burger joint without getting silly. Lots of wood and red leather and this sort of feel like the Middle Ages meets sixties family place.

Valerie got a mushroom burger, well done, and I got a mug for my *sanguine.* She looked a little put off, but it wasn't as if she hadn't seen it back at the Club, and I wasn't biting off the neck or anything like I did around Carl.

I may just be a dumb jock, but I do have some manners. "First time dating a vampire, huh?"

Valerie looked at the *sanguine* in my mug, which really was blood for all intents and purposes, then looked away. "Yeah, I guess." She glanced back, watching as I drank my alchemical blood. "Wouldn't you rather be biting me on the neck or something?"

I grinned and licked off my blood moustache. "Sure. I wouldn't have minded biting you even before I became a vampire. But three bites—that's all it takes. And trust me, you don't want to be a vampire."

"I'm certain of that . . ." she said under her breath. She probably didn't think I heard her, but I did, and I saw her give a little shudder too.

My guess was that she was a little vampophobic and had gone all Politically Correct and decided to get over it by dating an actual vampire. Not that I was complaining. I took my dates where I could get them.

Valerie finished her burger and I finished my *sanquine* and we made light conversation about football and the USC-UCLA rivalry. I hadn't looked at a paper all evening, and I was glad of it. The nut with the croquet mallet had probably struck again, and the last thing I wanted to do was read about someone I knew getting their head whacked off.

We window-shopped a bit more after dinner, and Valerie suggested catching a show, but the last thing I wanted to do was stay in some darkened theatre while some nut ran around with a croquet stake with my name on it. I know I was getting paranoid, but my case had been written up in the papers about ten years back when Martin had decided to do the whole 'Rose Bowl Bloodbath' thing, and I made a pretty big target.

"Why don't we go back to your place then?" Valerie asked at last.

She wasn't a vampire, so I didn't have to worry about inviting her in if things didn't turn out right, and as I said earlier, I couldn't really blame her for not inviting me back to her place on a first date. So I shrugged. "Sure. Sounds like a plan." I levitated a few inches. "Care to fly the friendly Jack?"

She hesitated. "Why don't we take a cab instead? It's—a little cool, and I didn't bring a jacket."

She was vampophobic alright, but was doing a good job of hiding it. "Sure thing."

At least horses aren't as skittish around vampires as they are around werewolves and ghosts. We were able to get cab pretty easy and take it back to Venice, and had a chance to talk a bit more on the way.

"My work takes me lots of places," Valerie said. "London, Rome, Mexico City—all over."

I shuddered. "I don't know which I'd rather go to less: Rome or Mexico. They stake my kind there."

"It's the Law of the Church."

I gave her a look. "And that makes it okay? Listen, Valerie, I don't like the idea of getting killed 'cause some senile old fart decides that I'm dead and that I don't have a soul. I may not have a fetch, and I don't cast a reflection, but that's not the same thing. I'm not a Catholic, and I don't give a flying fuck what the Pope thinks. I didn't elect him."

She smiled then. "I don't hold much with the Pope either. I'm Lutheran."

I grinned. "Must be lapsed if you're dating a vampire."

She smiled back. "I suppose so."

The cab got to my apartment and dropped us off. "Just a sec'," I said and slipped in through the keyhole. I checked the place out inside. Good thing—Carl had taken the hint, and he and Charlie were nowhere to be seen. I lit up a few candles and opened the door. "Welcome," I said. "Here's hoping that you can extend the invitation to me sometime."

Valerie didn't take the hint, but did come in, looking around the apartment. "It's—nice. Very bachelor." She reached into her purse then and did something with the door, and the next thing I knew there was a rosary dangling from the doorknob, the cross right over the keyhole.

There was another cross in Valerie's hand, a fucking silver crucifix in fact, and I was slammed back into the wall by the thing's aura. "I'm sorry, Jack," she said. "You were probably a decent man in life, since some of that seems to have carried over into this mockery. I'm sorry I wasn't quick enough to save you this pain. But at least I'll save others from sharing your torment."

"Holy shit," I said. "You're that nutcase."

She was getting the croquet stake out with the other hand and her eyes were gleaming with a weird light. "I'm Sister Mary Francesca of the Order of the Blessed Resurrection, and it is my duty to see you to your rest."

I shook my shades off and tried to lock eyes with her, but Valerie, or Sister Mary Francesca, or whatever her fucking name was, was absolutely bonkers and there was no way a vampire's Fascination could grab her attention. "Valerie!" I shouted. "Stop!"

"Do not try to speak my name, wicked one. This is not holy ground and it is not the Witching Hour and you may not use that power against me."

"What the fuck are you talking about?"

Sister Mary Francesca of the Order of the Blessed Croquet Mallet walked forward, stake raised, and I think she was about to bean me with J— with the guy nailed to her cross. "Do not speak as if you do not know your power, Child of Satan! You may walk onto the holy ground of the Cathedral during the hours when the church services lie unsaid, and if you gain the steeple and read forth the names of those within the village, they will die one by one, victims to your foul power!"

"What?" I said. "You're afraid I'm going to climb up to the top of St. V's with a copy of the Los Angeles white pages? And read the entire thing in three hours? You're fucking nuts, lady!"

"Enough of your lies, Spawn of Darkness!" She waved the crucifix at me, plastering me to the wall. "Our Father, who art in Heaven, Hallowed be Thy Name. . . ."

The prayer and all the Names of Power burnt my ears, holding me pinned.

"By Kingdom Come, Thy Will be done, On Earth as is in Heaven . . ."

"Someone—help me!" It was as close a prayer as I could get, but it must have worked, 'cause that was when Carl came in, knocking the rosary off the door, and making Sister Mary Francesca of the Fucked-Up Theology turn and point her crucifix at Carl. "By the Power of Jesus!" she shouted, and I swear, the Crown of Thorns popped off the J-Guy's head and went and hit Carl right in the chest.

He slammed back into the door, his glasses flying, and his eyes went glassy.

But my former date, and the current Croquet Mallet Murderer, had turned away from me, and as I said, I used to play football for USC. I saw my opening and literally went for a flying tackle, slamming Valerie to the floor. The silver crucifix burnt my chest where I held it to her, then she shouted, "By the Power of Jesus!"

I think I said that Carl had the Evil Eye, and Valerie had been taking it square-on. The curse fulfilled itself almost immediately, 'cause the new little Crown of Thorns shot straight up the way the crucifix was pointing and buried itself in Valerie's throat.

I rolled off, patting at the smoking brand on my chest, then looked over at Carl. He was lying back slumped against the door, his eyes shut tight and blood bubbling up from between his lips. He was breathing heavy, and blood oozed out of his chest where the crown had struck him.

"And that's a wrap," said a voice, and I looked over and saw Charlie stepping out of the mirror. "Congratulations, Carlos. You made it to Doomsday, and you get to die a hero."

"Stay away from him!" I shouted. "He's not dead!"

"Yet," finished Charlie. The fetch looked at his watch. "Give him another ten minutes and he's a goner. Trust me. I know." Charlie grinned like an imp.

"You can save him," I said. "Go get help. He can't go until you take him."

"And why would I want to do that, Jack? This is what we fetch's live for. And you won't believe how happy that girl's was to finally finish up business with her." He pointed to the corpse of Valerie, the former Croquet Mallet Murderer. "And there's about to be another happy fetch real soon now."

"Over my dead body!" I stood up and took a swing at Charlie.

My fist went right through him and he laughed. "Try again, vampire. You ain't got no fetch, so you can't touch me!"

I went and sat down next to Carl, holding his hand. "It's okay, buddy. It's going to be okay."

"I lit a candle for you, Jack," Carl murmured. More blood oozed out of his lips and I felt my fangs slide out. He was delirious, and his hand was getting as cold as mine.

As cold as mine.

I lifted up Carl's wrist and bit down hard, taking a sip of what little blood he had left.

"What in the Hell are you doing?" Charlie shrieked. His phantom hands waved through me, but I couldn't touch him, and he couldn't touch me.

I lowered Carl's wrist and licked my fangs. "I'm killing you, Charlie. Three bites from the vampire and Carl becomes one of the undead. And you die." I looked at the two holes in Carl's wrist. "That's one."

"Stop it, Jack! They'll kill you if you make another vampire!"

I moved Carl's sleeve up for a spot higher on his arm. "They'll kill me anyway, Charlie. I killed Valerie. Doesn't matter that she was a nut who was going to kill me."

"She killed herself," Charlie said. "She shot herself with her own wand. Jim knows. You'll get off free."

"I'm gonna save Carl anyway." I bit Carl a second time, drinking a little bit deeper, letting the curse take a firmer hold. I raised my fangs. "That's two. You want me to make it three? Or are you gonna go get help?"

Charlie looked around, but I know he knew I was serious. "This is blackmail, you know."

"So sue me."

Charlie glared. "I'm going to get him one day, you know. All you're doing is prolonging his suffering. And I promise you—He will suffer for this. You will too."

"And so will you, Charlie, unless you go get help."

"Okay, Jack," the fetch said. "You win. This time."

He stepped back into the mirror and disappeared around the corner.

Charlie was good to his word. Carl did suffer, 'cause he lay there in my arms for about two hours until the healer's came.

Charlie didn't take his soul in all that time, so the thauma-turgists had a hell of a time reanimating Carl, though not as bad as they would if Charlie had taken the soul. Luckily, with all the healing, the bite marks on Carl's arm got covered up, and Carl had been too far gone to remember much of what happened. And I wasn't telling, except that I said that I'd *threatened* to bite Carl, and so far as the law went, it wasn't illegal to threaten, so long as the person being threatened was a fetch, and Carl didn't want to press charges.

There was a big to-do over Valerie's death, but it came out okay. I got off with probation, since even the judge had to admit that I didn't need my vampiric abilities to do a flying tackle. And if some serial killer got whammied by the Evil Eye, then shot herself in the throat with her own crucifix, well . . .

The tabloids ate it up.

As for the rest of it, Carl and I are both okay, and back at the Club, and even Charlie's there too, though he's pretty sulky. Jim's also filing a class action suit on behalf of the Valerie's victims to get a necromancer to summon up her shade and get her to tell where she stashed the heads. The police are looking for them too, but I have more faith in Jim and the necromancers than I do the LAPD.

And that's about it. It sucks being cursed, but when you're all in it together, it's a little bit easier to get by.

Even with guys like Charlie.

# Vympyre

## WILLIAM F. NOLAN

*Even
the weariest
river . . .*

LOOD. MY OWN. Sweet Christ, my own! Seeping along my chest, soaking my white pullover, a spreading patch of dark red. So this is how it finally ends? With the stake being driven in another inch, each blow of the hammer like a thunderclap . . . closing my eyes in Paris with blood everywhere on the tumultuous streets, tasting it on my cool lips, with the guillotine hissing down, severed heads thumping wicker baskets . . . King Richard there (was it the Third Crusade?), his battle axe cleaving through the enemy's shoulder, sundering down through muscle, bone, and gristle, and watching the stricken rider topple from the tall back of the sweating gray horse . . . in Germany's Black Forest, barefoot, my flesh lacerated by thorn and stone, pursued by the shouting villagers, the flames of their torches wavering, flickering through the trees, a strange, surreal glow . . . gulls above the sunswept English Channel as I lower my head toward the child's white, delicately tender throat, with the warm sweet wine of her blood on my tongue. (So many myths about us. They call us creatures of the night, but many of us do not fear the bright sun. In truth, it cannot harm us, although we often hunt at night . . . so many myths) . . . on the high seat of the carriage, pitching and plunging through moonlit Edinburgh, wheels in thunderous clatter over the narrow, cobbled streets, hatless, my cape blown wild behind me as I lash at the straining team . . . the impossibly pink sands of the beach, with a stout sea wind rattling the palm fronds, the waves blood-colored, sunset staining the edge of horizon sky and the young woman's drugged, open, waiting flesh, and my lips drawn back, the needled penetration, and the lost cry of release . . . the limo driver's rasping voice above the surging current of Fifth Avenue traffic, recounting the intensity of the police hunt, and my quiet smile there with my back against the cool leather, invincible, the girl's corpse where no one can ever find it, with the puncture marks raw and stark on her skin . . . the stifling, musky darkness of the cave, the rough grained face of the club against my cupped fingers, the fetid tangle of beard cloaking my face, my lips thick and swollen, the hot roar of the saber-tooth still echo-sharp in my mind, and thinking not of the dead, drained female beside me but of the brute eyes of the beast . . . the stench of war, of cannon-split corpses, the blue-clad regiment sprawled along the slope, the crackling musket fire in the cool air of Virginia, the stone wall ahead of me in the rushing smoke . . . the plush gilt of the Vienna opera house, the music rising in a brassy tide and the tall woman beside me in blood-red velvet as I watch the faint heartbeat in the hollow of her arching throat, flushed ivory from the glow of stage lamps . . . the bitter-smoked train pulling into crowded Istanbul station, the towers of ancient Byzantium rising around me, the heavy leather suitcase bumping my leg, the thick wool suit pressing against my skin, the assignation ahead with the dark-haired little fool who trusts me . . . the bone-shuddering shock along my right arm as my sword sparks against the upthrust shield, the gaunt Christian falling back under the fury of my attack, the orgasmic scream of the Roman crowd awaiting another death . . . the long, baked sweep of sun-blazed prairie, suddenly quiet now after the vast drumming of herded buffalo, the young, pinto-mounted Indian girl riding easily beside me, with the flushed red darkness of her skin inviting me, challenging me . . . standing with Rameses II among the fallen Hittites, with the battle-thirst raging through me like a fever, the sharp odor of spilled blood everywhere, soaking deep into parched Egyptian sands . . . the reeking London alehouse along the Thames, the almond-eyed whore in my lap, giggling, her breath foul with drink, her blood-rich neck gleaming in the smoky light . . . the slave girl in Athens, kneeling in the dirt at my booted feet, begging me to spare her wretched life as the pointed tip of my sword elicits a single drop of crimson from her fear-taut throat . . . at the castle feast, soups spiced with sage and sweet basil, the steaming venison on platters of chased silver, the hearty wines of Auvergne aglow in jeweled flagons, with the Queen facing me across the great table, my eyes on the pale blue tracery of veins above the ruffled lace at her neck . . . and, at last, here—with all the long centuries behind me, their kaleidoscopic images flickering across my mind—hunted and found, trapped like an animal under a fog-shrouded sun along the soft Pacific shore, in this fateful year of one thousand nine-hundred ninety-two, as the ultimate anvil-ringing stroke of the hammer sends the stake deep into my rioting heart . . . to a sudden, unending darkness.

The final blood is mine.

# The Captive Angel

## S. P. SOMTOW

*A haunting tale*
*of a vampire*
*in flight . . .*

*In the excerpt from the third "Vampire Junction" novel which follows, Angel Todd, who has traded souls with vampire rock star Timmy Valentine in order to escape his trauma-ridden life, has been trapped inside a perfume vial by a Siamese shaman. Lady Chit, a Thai aristocrat, is traveling to Germany to join her husband, a member of the entourage that is accompanying Timmy Valentine on his world tour. On the flight, Angel's imprisoned soul speaks to her in her dreams, and tells her about his first day of being a vampire.*

*flying*

IGHT OVER ASIA: she was overcome by drowsiness yet could not sleep for a long time even though there was no one in the first-class cabin with her. Lauren was supposed to have come with her, but after the conflagration at the temple he had gone into a deep depression; he hadn't even been able to work on the painting of the dead whore standing in the window in the rain.

Now and then a stewardess shuffled past her aisle seat, poured her another glass of that insipid airline Beaujolais; Lady Chit had one eye on the movie—it was *Jurassic Park*—while in her earphones thrummed an easy listening adaptation of *Vampire Junction*. The cognitive dissonance did not inspire sleep. Nor did the dull ache in her breast, where the gash left by Angel Todd's bite had never entirely healed. It pained her now as she leaned back in the great leather seat and toyed with the controls of the stereo, switching from Pavarotti to k.d. lang to Kurt Cobain to Tori Amos and (by a sudden flick of the wrist) back to the familiar strains of Timmy Valentine.

It was disorienting to watch women being gassed in black and white while listening to the saccharine harmonies of

Timmy's early music, the songs she'd loved as a teenager back in the New Wave days. Then she remembered that Timmy had once told her that he too had been gassed once, in Auschwitz, because they thought he was a gipsy . . . though he had not, of course, been killed, since he had not yet achieved mortality.

A pang in her breast; not dull like all the others, but sharp, urgent; she was reliving it, the fang penetrating the soft skin. She touched herself through the silk of her blouse. It was throbbing, definitely throbbing, and with each throb a stab of pain. She reached in her purse for a Valium. Flying west, the nights are longer anyway, she thought, and now this.

As she groped in her purse, she came upon the perfume phial. . . .

Why did I bring the damn thing with me anyway? she thought. Even though the ajarn had told her to wear it next to her skin, she had disobeyed him after the first couple of nights of sleeplessness . . . she had tossed and turned and heard at her window a sound like the beating of great wings. And she had turned to her dwindling supply of Halcion and Valium to get her through the night.

But she couldn't throw it out either. After all, it contained . . . could you really call it a soul, when a vampire has no soul? But it was some kind of essence, some part of what had once been Angel Todd.

She was looking at it again now. She was shaking though there was no turbulence and the sky outside the window was clear and cloudless and studded with stars. You could not see the original faux ivory; she had had it encased in silver down at the mall, and the ajarn had bound it tighter with a mantra of entrapment. It was warm to the touch. She could feel pressure against her palm . . . like a caterpillar in a jumping bean . . . like a baby kicking in the womb.

Then she heard the whisper in her mind:

*Please don't put me away I need to feel you I need to touch your skin I need you I want you I need you to feel me*

She put the phial down quickly.

It plunked into the airline Beaujolais, and the red wine fizzed a little.

I know, she thought, you "nevairrr drink . . . wine."

She fished it out and dried it off and popped one more Valium. This time it better damn well work, she thought. And it did.

Except that, stirring a little, an hour or so later, she felt an unwonted weight around her neck, a hunk of hot metal wedged against her breast, the stickiness from her once more oozing stigma. . . .

Then she fell . . . no, rather she plummeted headlong into sleep, a deeper, darkner sleep than she had experienced in many months . . . and, sleeping, she saw Angel Todd once again . . . just as she had last seen him . . . on the threshold of undeath . . . waiting.

*\*dreaming\**

Listen to me. Listen. Listen.

Another time. Another soul.

You have to listen to me because you're the one who caged me inside of silver and imitation ivory. All that I am is in here until you set me free. Bitch! You tricked me. I needed you and you fucking tricked me. I came to you because I thought you'd understand. In a way, you *do* understand. That's why you got me here with you. I've touched the inside of you and your blood is in me and I know that even though you're afraid of me there's a part of you that loves me now with a love that's buried so deep inside you it's like a dead body festering in a grave. That's me. I'm your angel, your evil angel.

In this phial there's no time and no space. Everything that ever happened to me is happening again, all at the same time. I want you to see it with me. That's why I'm sending deep into your dreams. So you'll see. So you'll believe. So you'll know why you're going to set me free.

Look! Look! It's the moment of my becoming.

Look again! See me without seeing. Touch me without touching.

*vampire junction*

You can say that life is a journey on a choo-choo train where you can't choose where to get on or off. You can't pick first class or baggage train or squatting in the tender with the coal dust choking you. You can say that every life is a train trip. But most lives don't pass through Vampire Junction.

Most lives, when they end, they go into a tunnel and they never come out. The tunnels don't go nowhere and they don't end, they just, you know, they're just tunnels. But you know that me and some of my friends have been through that tunnel and came out the other side only we weren't the same no more. Think back. We were in all caught up in the big dream together . . . you and me and Timmy and Brian and Petra and many of our friends . . . and then we were on the train . . . and one by one, you all got off . . . you went back to the real world. And finally there's only me, and Brian and Petra, and they're the ones that truly love me, and we're all like some kind of satanic version of Mary and Joseph and Jesus, you know. They want to nurture me. They're ready to throw away their humanness and go with me. It's a awesome feeling. They're hovering over me. They cocoon me from the darkness as we start trundling into that big old tunnel. They shelter me with their bodies and I don't have to look out of the window at the great black nothing that is all that the tunnel is.

And the tunnel goes and on and on and I'm scared shitless at first even though this is what I chose to be, what I've always longed for. But it's not the way I imagined it, no way. I'm all thinking: This is it, I've ditched my live and I'm gonna start over as a vampire and it'll all be one long party . . . yeah, I saw *Lost Boys* and after I met Timmy Valentine I knew that wasn't all there was to being a vampire but I guess I still had this party feeling about going down into the darkness, but then it's like it goes on and on and on and time stands still and it ain't just the darkness and the loneliness but shit it's *boring* too, just moving on and on . . . and I'm starting to think . . . maybe there is no light . . . maybe there is no end to this. Maybe my death is just a plain-wrap death like any other death, a death that goes on forever.

Brian comforts me and Petra hugs me . . . but you know . . . I don't feel nothing. I can barely hear them talking. I hide myself inside them.

And then one day . . . can't really say *one* day 'cause there ain't no day here . . . I start to dig my way out. It's because of the hunger that started when I first began this journey . . . it started as a tingling feeling, like the prick of a painkiller injection . . . but now it's a huge and overwhelming thing that screams in my mind and doesn't let me think and all I want to do is make it go away but it gets bigger and bigger and finally it's as big as the blackness I'm traveling through . . . and I try to hold it in but at last it snaps and I don't know what I'm doing, I have to devour something, I don't know what, I feed and feed and feed and feed and then, suddenly, all at once, the train . . .

. . . has burst through the darkness and around me's all like, cornfields and shit . . . a sea of silver under the moonlit sky. And the hunger has popped . . . kind of like a zit . . . and I'm all peaceful again . . . all peaceful . . . and then I look around for Brian and Petra . . . and the train rattles as it curves along the bank of a gleaming river . . . I hear the train . . . I hear the crickets . . . I even hear the corn push up oh God so slowly through the packed dung and mud . . . but I don't hear Brian and Petra . . . until I understand that when they enveloped me with their love and protection it wasn't just *like* a cocoon, it was a cocoon . . . I ate my way out . . . by being born I had to devour . . . first the ones who loved me most and then myself . . . my own flesh . . . my own soul . . . I had to remake myself . . . in a new image . . . not life, but life's mirror . . . not death, but something deeper . . . oh God it scares me shitless because now I no one and I'm just this lost kid sitting on a train going to shit knows where and the train don't even have a train driver because the train is me, my life, my death, taking me to places no kid should ever see . . . oh Jesus I think I'm gonna cry and then guess what I fucking can't, I can't cry anymore and I can't even remember how the hot tears used to feel on my cheeks like, when my mother touched me under the sheets with her breath smelling of liquor like, when I couldn't get the song right and I thought they were going to kill me like, when I saw my brother lowered into the green earth like, when I begged Timmy Valentine to steal my soul away.

Don't even know if I'll ever get off this train . . . don't even know if I'll ever stand on something that ain't vibrating and clanging. We're whipping through station after station too fast to read their names. One time I think I see my mother standing in a churchyard but no, it's some other woman in a night dress with one foot in, one out of a half-dug grave, and another time I see couple other people I know they're really dead I mean like, people I sort of knew on the movie set when it was burning down.

The whistle and the brakes: screaming.

We stop.

I can smell my native earth.

It's Hangman's Holler.

*love and death*

I start walking and after a while I figure I don't have to walk. I kind of let go and the wind half drags me half embraces me. The wind is even inside me because the stuff I'm made of ain't flesh exactly . . . it's the fabric of people's nightmares. People believe in me. That's why I'm real. Timmy told me that once. "You'll be an archetype," he said. Whatever the fuck that is. He's had two thousand years of book-learning and I'm just a dumb hick that happens to be the spitting image of him.

Okay so I feel myself kind of half melting letting the wind and me take up the same space because I'm not totally in *this* space at all . . . *and I* drift. Hangman's Holler. Floating uphill. The grass is black in the moonlight and it's swimming in dew. I know where I'm going I guess. Past the church where Damien Peters used to preach before he got himself the fancy bible-banging empire. Past Mr. Flagstad's general store with its broken pane that ain't been fixed all of my life. Oh yeah. I'm not alive no more. Wooden houses with beat-up pickups parked alongside lean-to mailboxes. Fences that trail off nowheres, weeds strutting up through broken concrete. I know this place so fucking well it would hurt if I could feel hurt.

The house on the hill: abandoned. Broken windows and the wind's blowing. We left that house when we drove out west and we never looked back and we never even locked it up cause there's nothing in it a body'd want to steal. Shit, it hasn't changed none, except for wasting away from not being tended to.

There's the hillock where we buried my twin brother Errol. Because only one of us could survive. "The two of you'd have been the death of me," my momma said to me once. And then we never spoke about it again.

I listen.

There's a rat running around in the mattress of the old bed I used to lay in. There's cockroaches shuffling in the walls. I can hear them. I can hear Mr. Flagstad grunting in his sleep. I can hear Mrs. Flagstad snoring. There's a cat curling up in a trash can lid somewheres, a slick lick, tongue across fur.

That's when I understand that I can *really* hear now, hear for the first time. To be human is to be color-blind to the billion hues of sound. Behind the crickets, behind the gropings under cotton sheets, I hear the grass grow . . . a deep sighing that's the bass note of the big old thundering chord that's echoing in the wet wind . . . too deep for a human to grasp . . . and I know that if you can't hear the bass note, what's holding up the music? It's just noise. The music of mortals is just a mote of harmony struggling to stay alive in a humungous sea of discord. *They don't hear the music!* I'm telling myself. And that's the first discovery about what's changed for me.

Now I'm listening to the music for the first time.

And I understand a lot of shit I never understood before too. Like in Timmy's songs, sometimes there'd seem to be like, a missing piece, a hole in the texture . . . part of what *Rolling Stone* called a "wayward eccentricity of structure." But now I see that those are holes for hearing the echo of the universe

. . . not just the grass growing and the whispering wind but even things that make no sound, like the planets hurtling through the empty spaces and the galaxies exploding a jillion light years away . . . if only you have ears to hear, you can know that every one of them songs has got like a piece of the life and death of the whole frigging universe in it. So now I know what Timmy's music was really about.

It ought to take my breath away but I don't breathe no more.

That's when I hear my name

*You a angel*

on the wind, coming from uphill somewheres . . . and I know whose voice it is, calling for me out of the human past. It's Becky Slade. She used to say that to me . . . you *a angel Angel* . . . the only black girl in my homeroom at Col. Sinclair Junior High . . . it's the same voice again maybe a little huskier maybe not and the only difference is I can hear it carried on the night wind and it's coming from farther uphill, farther than a human can hear. Maybe this is why the train has left me here, so I can start off at the same place where I started in my human life. Maybe I have to revisit my old life before I can start again. Or maybe it's just that the old place still clings to me . . . like the earth sticks to your skin when you're climbing out of a fresh-dug grave.

There's a barn where me and Becky used to go sometimes and that's where we went when she wanted to show me what she looks like when she's naked. And she wanted to see me too. That place where she showed me what a boy can do to a girl except that I'd already learned it from my mother. . . .

*You a angel!*

She's there in that secret place and I ain't and I don't rightly know how I feel about that. No one was supposed to know about that place. The wind howls. I start to lope uphill and soon I'm more flying than walking because my body is shifting shape so it'll be more streamlined in the wind . . . what am I now? A bat, a raven? I don't know except that the wind picks me up and when I spread my arms I catch the moonlight, my feathers glisten, I tumble along the currents of the air.

*angel*

and yes. I'm black. I'm beautiful. I sweep. I soar. I screech and wheel across the silver moon

*angel*

hearing her tart voice, a raven, ravening. She's saying, *I use to come here with Angel you know the one he use to be called Angel but now he's Timmy Valentine. Ain't bullshitting you. At the Oscars. You watch them Oscars didn't you? but he wasn't just a movie star he was something special to me, the onliest boy that didn't call me nigger to my face. And we use to come here to this barn and he touched me, don't be getting jealous now, there wasn't much to it he was so ignorant about what to do, like a little child and all, sleep ever' single night in the same bed with his momma, I think she made him all twisted up inside wrapped him up inside of her fat flesh made it so he couldn't even you know, pop a boner, he shriveled up inside when I tried to . . . he like a little snail coiling back up inside his shell, and I say to him, Are you afraid? well when you bigger, when you not afraid no more, you come back and see Becky Slade and she jump your bones, baby. And you know what, I think he scared. Then I watch him on them Oscars and was almost like he wasn't the same person no more. He look right out at me from inside of the television set and I look into his eyes and I think this ain't the same Angel Todd no more. I done lost him. He still a boy but not the boy I play with in the barn not the boy I said to him You a angel Angel.*

Then there's another voice. *Don't talk about that bullshit baby.*

Whose voice? I can't tell but it trips the rhythm of my flying and now I'm falling out of the sky like a stone, now suddenly I'm in a closed space, the smell of cowshit, dry grass, old wood, peeling paint, must have just funneled in through the cracks in the walls, and I'm perched in the rafters of a big old barn and I see her from way up, see her eyes first, two polished smoky quartzes in that gloom.

*Angel* she says but not to me.

The boy that's with her, tall slender black glistening with his pants around his ankles, don't talk much, just touching her. Don't like the way he smells, don't like his musky sweat, cause I smell every hormone that's racing through his blood, know he's young and all he can think about is pounding that bitch till he comes, not paying her no mind at all except like a piece of meat.

And so I'm spreading my wings again, sending the straw flying from the roof beams, wavery raven shadow over their heads, but I reach a pool of shadow just beyond where they're sitting and I can't go no further. It's like battering against a force field. In a moment I understand why. It's the invitation thing. Gotta be invited. I should know that from all the fucking vampire movies I seen when I was alive.

But I gotta talk to her. She's gotta know that he's just using her up, she's nothing more than prey to him, all he wants is to suck her dry, just like, just like—

*A vampire.*

I flap and flap against the penumbra of hay. But she won't know it's me unless I—

Change. Transform. Flow outward, fill the shadow air with the image of what I used to be.

*Angel!*

And she's seen me, no she's seen an image kindled by her

memories: me, twelve years old, torn jeans, muddy blonde hair, big eyes; I'm standing at the edge of the force field and when she calls my name, the way she calls me with that faint promise of an invitation is enough to make the force field start to thaw and I can feel it soften and I'm swimming through like a bee through honey; and the boy looks up and sees no one because he has no image to fasten onto; but Becky looks at me and her brown eyes fill with longing and I know that I'm the onliest one she truly loved and that fills me with, I don't know, the ghost of a long-dead feeling; and she says to the boy, "Look. He came back after all. Maybe I didn't lose him. Maybe Angel remember Becky Slade."

"Let me come to you," I say. Knowing the words are double-edged and they can never be free from deceit, because I don't have a soul no more, and I can't love.

"Come," she says. And the barrier shatters and I'm standing right there, Becky on my right leaning against a pile of straw, the dude on my left, pulling up his boxers.

"Come and get me, motherfucker," he says, and puts up his fists.

"Angel," says Becky. For a moment I think I'm feeling what it was like to be a human being, to have my blood flushing my cheeks, my heart pounding, my dick getting all hard and then that feeling fades away and all I'm left with is that yawning hunger and I don't know what to do and I say, "Becky, get away from me," and she says, with kind of a half-smile in her voice, "Why Angel, you become so high and mighty now that you rich? Did you think I was going to wait for you?" and I don't have an answer for her. I want to hold my memories but they are crumbling to dust. There's only the hunger. I don't even hear what she's saying.

The tall black dude slams his fists into my chest but I make myself hard, like eternity. His hands shatter. He screams. Blood sprays my face. It reddens the pallor of my cheeks and I can taste it on my lips and now the hunger's really driving me and I can't help myself no more, I just kind of surround him and swallow him up and spit him out, a desiccated sack of skin and bone, and all his blood just kind of sponges into me, not just through my fangs but nostrils, my eyes, even the pores of my skin . . . all at once dude, all at once, it's almost too much for me to take . . . my eyes redden. I look like a movie vampire now with the gore dribbling from the corners of my lips. And you know Becky just looks up and doesn't speak and it's like she's been waiting for this moment all her life. Doesn't she understand them memories mean nothing no more? What does she see when she looks at me? Timmy used to tell me that people see the things they're most afraid of. But she don't seem frightened.

She crosses over to me. She's naked and dark as the night. She hasn't grown much. Her breasts are shallow and her hips still narrow. There's only one naked bulb swaying over the piles of straw. She smells of her boyfriend's armpits. But beneath that smell there's the sweet odor of her baby blood. She tramples the dead boy's limp skin. It's like he never existed. She looks into my eyes and she says, "I always knew you was an angel, Angel."

"I'm not an angel, Becky. I'm . . . a monster."

"Monsters don't be beautiful like you."

"Ain't beautiful inside, Becky. Not any more. Something happened to me. You don't know how much I wanted to get away from my life . . . momma choking the life out of me in that sweaty bed . . . a life where everything was just pretend. I could hear Errol, my twin brother, calling to me every night out of the dead earth, and I wanted to be like Timmy Valentine because no one could hurt him and he was for ever. But it turned out he wanted to be me. So we became each other. Except . . . I guess it didn't work. Not all the way. Don't come near me, Becky, I'm a vampire."

"Bullshit. You think you the only one who wants to get away. You think you the only one that get hisself shit on. It a thousand times worse for me. You got out of this fucking town. You got yourself money and fame. Becky Slade, she stay here. Nothing to look forward to in Hangman's Holler, Angel Todd, nothing but growing old and dying."

And she's saying these words and damn it she's still so fucking young but her eyes are as old as Timmy Valentine's; and I know that I've come for her, that I am her hope and her redemption; and I know that her hope and her redemption are false.

But she takes one more step toward me. Jesus I can smell her blood. It smells of the grave. Already.

"Fuck me," Becky Slade says. "you always wanted to and then you thought about your momma and you couldn't get hard, don't think I didn't know, everyone at school talked about how you and Marjorie slept in the same bed and shit, don't you be thinking it a dark secret like inside a romance book. Now she's dead and you can."

"But I'm dead too."

"Then if you can't fuck me, do whatever it is you do. Kill me, I don't give a shit. Pop me with a straw and suck the grape juice out of me, cause I don't want to be Becky Slade no more."

And we're both standing on the dead boy. I crush his skull with my heel and grind his bones into the floor planks, and the naked light bulb swings in a little circle, and she puts her arms around me and I see that to her I'm intense and burning cold and hard and full of passion but to me she is I don't know, nothing more than the ghost of long-dead feelings and yes there is the blood than rushes through her roaring like whitewater like a cataract like the rapids in the hills behind the house where my mother took me into her sagging body and lowered my dead brother into the ground and swallowed pills like handfuls of M&Ms and all those memories are in the screaming of her blood because her blood is a thread that ties me to that past I've tried so hard to escape except that there is no escape because the past I hate so much has inside of it all the things I remember how to love. I didn't mind killing the other one, he didn't mean nothing to me you know, but killing Becky Slade is what would have been making love for me if I was still alive. I guess I never got to make love, really. I only fucked. I mean, was fucked. Now I am making love for the first time. First a gentle pinprick in the fingertip, just a couple drops squeezed from the capillaries, silky on my tongue, then I'm probing a little further, biting into the arm, sending an icy pleasure shuddering through her, feeling the pulse quicken against my quivering teeth, then all the way up the arm, the two tiny holes on either side of the jugular, not quite piercing it because she doesn't want to die right away, she wants to go on looking at me, drinking death out of my eyes, and so I'm moving in and out of her not in some vulgar human way, dick in cunt, nothing so dirty, just my lips and my tongue teasing the dark blood out of her, well at first it's just teasing but then I start to suck harder and she feels how urgently I need her and she thrusts hard against me and I feel her dusky flesh against me and I feel the heartbeats pounding and I reach through the flesh, invade the thousand-branching web of vein and artery, I go inside of her, not just the womb but all of her and at the center of her there is the heart and it shivers as I rip the ribcage open and part the lungs and there it is, still pumping, but more weakly now because the pleasure is too much for her . . . I bury my face inside her flesh and the blood sluices from her, splashes my cheeks . . . I'm snorting blood, blood is running in my ears, in the space between my eyeballs and their sockets, pouring down my throat . . . and for a moment I'm glimpsing, dimly, what it's like to be loved.

But the glimpse is fading.

Too soon, she's dead, and again I'm left with nothing.

Another emptiness. Another yearning.

I don't know what to do now. I've heard that I can make other vampires. But that gets complicated, don't it? I decide I'm just gonna burn down the barn. So I do that, and I fly into the night.

*flying*

Spiralling upward into the air now. It feels good, I think. Mostly I hear the wind but underneath I can hear Hangman's Holler sleeping. I see all the people living their dollhouse lives. Even my own house seems like one of those HO scale model Appalachian houses in Timmy Valentine's infinite train layout.

Look, there's the knoll where Errol's buried. There's a circlet of little trees that Momma had planted there when we got our first big check from Stupendous Entertainment. I remember I used to put my ear to the earth and think I could hear him call to me in his baby voice. The voice was echoey, you know, that *Poltergeist* sound effect, someone in the studio showed me how they do that, run it through a digital box, human in, ghost out . . . it's wild.

Suddenly I want to do that again, so I plummet down out of the sky, bird of prey now, beak out, wings unfurled against the silvery moon . . . I'm *bad*, dude, I'm *down*, that's how they made me talk in Hollywood, *lose that Kentucky twang or we'll lose the market share* . . . Now I'm on the ground, morphing to human form just when my claws collide with grass and stone.

The grass is tall here. It's like it was sucking extra chemicals out of the soil, organic fertilizer I guess. I know Errol's body must have been consumed a long time ago but maybe there's something still here, some piece of him, hovering around the place Momma put him.

I put my ear to the earth.

And you know . . . I can hear so fucking much, the itty-bitty earthworms chomping the soil and shitting it back out as they burrow, the crickets rubbing their legs together . . . but I can't hear my brother.

What's wrong? There was always something. Yeah, my imagination, my right brain, something, calling to me. Maybe it's because I don't have an imagination no more. I'm an imagined thing myself. I'm only real because so many people have watched so many vampire movies and made me into a true thing. I can't imagine. I can't dream.

Or maybe . . . its because life and death are linked together, flowing in and out of each other, a big old circle like PJ would say . . . and so the living can hear an echo of the dead, and the dead can whisper in the ears of the living . . . but what about me? I ain't alive and I ain't dead. I'm not part of the great cycle of infinity. I got through the cracks.

Yeah. It's all dawning on me now. Just how alone I am. Jesus is this what I bargained for prayed for exchanged souls with a vampire for? The hunger's still there. The boy I killed satisfied it for only a split second . . . Becky Slade a bit longer, because she was someone who used to feel for me when I was still alive. But now it's all come back. It will never go away.

There used to be a whole rainbow of emotions and now there's only one.

*Errol! My* scream is the cry of a vulture. But there's no carrion to feed on. Feverishly I'm clawing up the soil because I want to know if there's even a little piece of my family I can cling to. But there isn't. I can't even trust my memory. I'm not even sure if Errol ever lived, or if it's just a thing I saw in a mirror once, a fucked-up reflection of myself.

The emotions have gone from color to black-and-white.

No, it's worse than that. It's like the whole universe has become one humungous motherfucking video that I'm trapped in . . . some virtual reality thing . . . and everything I touch, taste, smell is hyper-vivid because it's all electronically pumped up and color-jazzed and juiced up with mega-intensities but . . . but . . . I still don't *really* touch, taste, smell . . . no . . . I don't feel a fucking thing . . . nothing, nothing . . . only the hunger.

## *flying*

The airplane was going through some kind of turbulence. Lady Chit stirred. A pang went through her chest and she saw that there was a small, dark, bloody stain where her bra had become plastered to the wound in her breast.

*Please,* came a still small voice in the back of her head. *Please, please, release me.*

She ransacked her purse and finally managed to dig out one last, dusty Valium. She swallowed it, and the rest of her wine, and once more tumbled down the well of nightmares. . . .

And still it was night over Asia; flying westward, time stretches; a night can seem forever.

About
the
Authors

# About the Authors

**JOHN GREGORY BETANCOURT** is the author of eleven science fiction and fantasy novels (including *Jonny Zed, the Blind Archer, Rememory* and *Rogue Pirate*). With his spouse, Kim, he runs the World Fantasy Award-nominated independent publishing company, The Wildside Press. He also claims Jean Stine was "largely responsible for my career today."

**JANRAE FRANK** is a well-known fantasy author and critic. Her fiction has appeared in anthologies like *Amazons* and *Dragon Tales*; her non-fiction in *The Washington Post, Movieline, Black Belt* and other publications. She is currently working on her first book, *Women At Arms: An Encyclopedia of Female Soldiers, Patriots and Spies*, due out from Facts on File in 1996.

**DIANA G. GALLAGHER**'s Hugo winning fan artwork hardly prepared readers for her novels of dark fantasy and horror. Her most recent works include *Arcade*, an entry in the young adult "Deep Space Nine" series, and adult fare like *The Alien Dark*. Her main hobby is trying not to be a sucker for dogs.

**E. J. GOLD** is a triple-threat man: science fiction writer, guru and fine artist. His science fiction includes such delicious send-ups as "Those Villains from Vega 8," his work on personal-transformation, the best-selling, *Lazy Man's Guide to Death and Dying*—while his paintings, ceramics and sculpture have adorned some of the world's most famous museums.

**ADRIENNE MARTINE-BARNES** is the author of such finely crafted fantasy novels as *The Chambered Nautilus, Dragon Rises, The Sea Sword*. With Diana Paxton she is the co-author of the delightful Fionn MacCumhal series. She is also a highly-talented craftswoman whose masks, quilts, spirit paintings and hand-dyed fabrics adorn many homes.

**DAWN MARTINEZ-BYRNE** describes herself as a costumer, Society for Creative Anachronism drop-out, and folk singer. She and her family also sell jewelry, costume items and swords at local science fiction conventions. She is a graduate of several writing workshops. "The Cage" is her first story.

**CHRIS MORAN**, a self-described "book-editing shamanic drag queen," is a former editor of *Whole Life* magazine. A small press specialist and trade book editor, Chris lives in Topanga Canyon, California, surrounded by a circle of "androgynes, gynanders, womyn-loving-womyn, and various friends of the wild and the night."

**KEVIN ANDREW MURPHY** has appeared in anthologies like *Wildcards* and *The King is Dead: Tales of Elvis Post Mortum*, as well as such distinguished publications as *Weird Tales* and *Midnight Zoo*. His passions and folklore, mythology and medieval alchemy. He is proudest of his contribution to *Weird Tales for Shakespeare*.

**WILLIAM F. NOLAN** is one of the Grand Old Men of horror. His reputation is equaled only by that of Ray Bradbury. Nolan is the author of 55 books, 112 short stories, 500 non-fiction pieces and over 40 television and film scripts. His novels include *Helltracks* and the Logan's Run trilogy.

**DARRELL SCHWEITZER** is a World Fantasy Award nominee author. He is also one of the field's most perceptive editors and critics. His novels include *We Are All Legends* and *The Shattered Goddess*. His stories have been collected in *Transients* and *Tom O'Bedlam's Night Out*.

**DAVID N. WILSON** is one writer who is at sea a lot of the time—with the U.S. Navy. This gives him plenty of leisure time with few distractions: an ideal environment for a writer. Not so surprisingly, he has become a productive short story writer whose work has appeared in genre magazines like *Cemetery Dance*, *Death Room* and *The Tomb*, and been selected for Best of The Year anthologies.

**S. P. SOMTOW** is the mysterious pseudonym of a very affable fellow, who just happens to be an award winner in several different genres of literature and fields of artistic endeavor. He is the author of a number of critically acclaimed horror novels including *Moon Dance* and *Vampire Junction*. His award-winning short stories have appeared in more than three dozen magazines and anthologies.

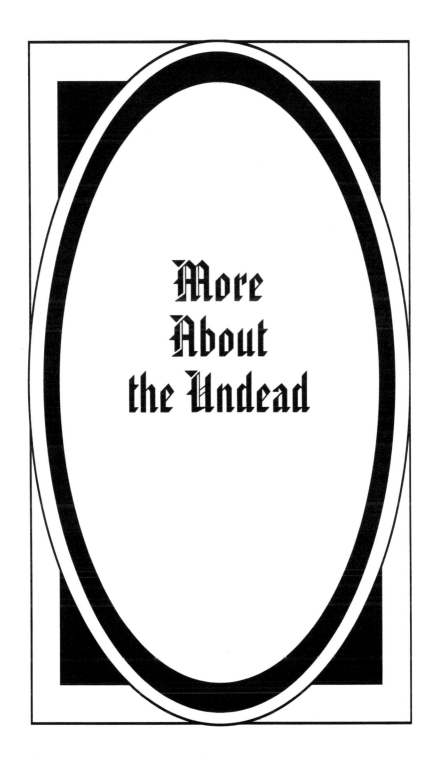

# More About the Undead

*(The editors believe readers whose thirst for the company of the undead is as yet unslaked might enjoy some or all of the following books and motion pictures.)*

## RECOMMENDED READING

## NOVELS

*Afterage*
Yvonne Navarro

*Anno Dracula*
Kim Newman

*The Black Castle*
Les Daniels

*Book of Common Dread*
Brent Monahan

*Carrion Comfort*
Dan Simmons

*Children of the Night*
Dan Simmons

*The Dark Angel*
Meredith Ann Pierce

*The Dracula Murders*
Philip Daniels

*Dracula Unborn*
Peter Tremayne

*Dracula Unbound*
Brian W. Aldiss

*Dracula's Diary*
Michael Geare & Michael Corby

*Empire of Fear*
Brian Stableford

*Fevre Dream*
George R. R. Martin

*The Hand of Dracula*
Robert Lory

*I Am Legend*
Richard Matheson

The Lestat Trilogy:
*The Vampire Lestat*
*Interview with the Vampire*
*Queen of the Damned*
Anne Rice

*Live Girls*
Ray Garton

*Nina*
Marie Kiraly

*Love Bite*
Sherry Gottlieb

*The Night Stalker*
Jeff Rice

*Night Thrust*
Patrick Whalen

The Saint-Germain Novels:
*Hotel Transylvania*
*The Palace*
*Blood Games*
*Tempting Fate*
Chelsea Quinn Yarbro

*Salem's Lot*
Stephen King

*Sybella, or The Blood Stone*
Tanith Lee

*They Thirst*
Robert R. McCammon

*Those Who Hunt the Night*
Barbara Hambly

*The Vampyre*
John William Polidori

*Vampire Junction*
S. P. Somtow

*Vampire Tapestry*
Suzi MacKee Charnas

*Vampires*
John Stakley

*Vampire's Moon*
Peter Saxon

*Varney the Vampyre, or The Feast of Blood*
James Malcom Rymer


## ANTHOLOGIES

*Dracula, Prince of Darkness*
Martin H. Greenberg (ed)

*Weird Vampire Stories*
Martin H. Greenberg (ed)

*Vampires: Two Centuries of Great Vampire Stories*
Allen Ryan

*Tomorrow Sucks*
Greg Cox (ed)

*A Feast of Blood*
Charles M. Collins (ed)

## RECOMMENDED VIEWING

## THE UNDEAD

Blacula

Blood & Roses

Bloodbath

Blood Fiend

Bloodsuckers

The Blood Drinkers

Captain Kronos, Vampire Hunter

Count Yorga

The Curse of Lemora

Curse of the Undead

Curse of the Vampires

Daughters of Darkness

The Fearless Vampire Killers

Forever Knight

The Hunger

Innocent Blood

Jonathan

Kiss of the Vampire

Lust for a Vampire

Lost Boys

Mark of the Vampire

Martin

My Son, the Vampire

Nosferatu

Nosferatu, The Vampire

Playgirls and the Vampire

Return of the Vampire

Salem's Lot: The Movie

A Taste of Blood

Terror In the Crypt

The Vampire

The Vampire & the Ballerina

The Vampire Lovers

The Vampire's Ghost

Vampire Circus

Vampire Hunter

Vampire

Vampyr


## DRACULA

Abbott & Costello Meet Frankenstein

Blood for Dracula

Blood of Dracula

Blood of Dracula's Castle

Bram Stoker's Dracula (1973)

Brides of Dracula

Count Dracula

Countess Dracula

Dracula (1931)

Dracula (1979)

Dracula (Spanish Version)

Dracula AD 1972

Dracula and the Legend of the
Seven Golden Vampires

Dracula Has Risen from the Grave

Dracula, Prince of Darkness

Dracula's Daughter

The Horror of Dracula

House of Dracula

Old Dracula

The Return of Dracula

Satanic Rites of Dracula

Scars of Dracula

Son of Dracula

Taste the Blood of Dracula

Tender Dracula

# If you enjoyed this Longmeadow Press Edition you may want to add the following titles to your collection:

| ITEM No. | TITLE | PRICE |
|---|---|---|
| 0-681-00525-4 | New Eves SCIENCE FICTION ABOUT THE EXTRAORDINARY WOMEN OF TODAY AND TOMORROW | 14.95 |
| 0-681-00693-5 | Bloodlines | 19.95 |
| 0-681-00725-7 | The Works of Jack London | 19.95 |
| 0-681-00687-0 | The Works of Nathaniel Hawthorne | 19.95 |
| 0-681-00729-X | The Works of H. G. Wells | 19.95 |
| 0-681-00795-8 | The Works of Henry David Thoreau | 19.95 |
| 0-681-00753-2 | Silver Screams: Murder Goes Hollywood | 8.95 |

Ordering is easy and convenient.
Order by phone with Visa, MasterCard, American Express or Discover:
☎ **1-800-322-2000,** Dept. 706
or send your order to:
Longmeadow Press, Order/Dept. 706,
P.O. Box 305188, Nashville, TN 37230-5188

Name _____

Address _____

City _____ State _____ Zip _____

| Item No. | Title | Qty | Total |
|---|---|---|---|
|  |  |  |  |
|  |  |  |  |
|  |  |  |  |
|  |  |  |  |

Check or Money Order enclosed Payable to Longmeadow Press — Subtotal

Charge: ❑ MasterCard   ❑ VISA   ❑ American Express   ❑ Discover — Tax

Account Number — Shipping — 2.95

Total

Card Expires

Signaure _____ Date _____

Please add your applicable sales tax: AK, DE, MT, OR, 0.0%—CO, 3.8%—AL, HI, LA, MI, WY, 4.0%—VA. 4.5%—GA, IA, ID, IN, MA, MD, ME, OH, SC, SD, VT, WI, 5.0%—AR, AZ, 5.5%—MO, 5.725%—KS, 5.9%—CT, DC, FL, KY, NC, ND, NE, NJ, PA, WV, 6.0%—IL, MN, UT, 6.25%—MN, 6.5%—MS, NV, NY, RI, 7.0%—CA, TX, 7.25%—OK, 7.5%—WA. 7.8%—TN, 8.25%